His Security

His Guardians Book 5

by

Ronna Bacon

Isaiah 54:17 No weapon that is formed against you shall be blessed; and every tongue that shall rise against you in judgment, you shall condemn. This is the inheritance of the servants of Jehovah, and their righteousness is from Me, says Jehovah.

Psalms 46:1 God is our refuge and strength, a very present help in trouble.

Table of Contents

Prologue

She watched as the young woman ran, fear chasing at her heels. She knew that she could catch her if she really wanted to, but she didn't. The timing wasn't right, not just yet. She looked over her shoulder, fear driving her actions. They were waiting for her, somewhere along the route and they wanted their money. She turned back to watch as the younger woman disappeared from view.

The younger woman checked once more over her shoulder. She could feel the person out there, had felt them there for weeks now. She didn't know who they were or what they wanted, but she didn't like the feeling that grew with each passing day. She could talk to the men in her life, but without a name or concrete proof she was being followed, it would do no good. All that would happen was that her own activities would be curtailed, and she would become a prisoner in her own home and vehicle.

She passed the man she dreaded seeing, hoping he didn't notice her. With relief, she got by him and around to her vehicle. Quickly, she pulled away and headed as far from there as she could in her town. Did she have to move to another town to have freedom and peace? She hoped not. Lord, please, bring them out into the open. Let me have the security of freedom once more.

Chapter 1

To say Leah MacGowan was tired, hungry and frustrated would have been the understatement of the year. She was headed home but had to make a stop first, and she really wasn't in the mood to talk with anyone, even if they were family. She had had enough of people today, and the day wasn't over yet.

She pulled the heavy tow truck she was driving to a stop in front of her aunt's home and looked at the driveway. Great, she thought. I have to drop this parcel off for Marg and they've got company. Not the way I wanted to end by day, Lord. I was hoping they'd be out and I could just drop the parcel and leave.

Ben Johnson, retired Riverville police detective, was ensconced in his favourite chair on his deck, talking with two members of Rebel's Elite Security Team, a local company that now specialized in training security teams. Ian Galbraith and Joseph Broderick were members of a men's Bible group at their church, and Ben and Marg always took opportunity to have members of the group over for meals. Ian's fiancée was away that day, and Ian was glad to have something to fill his time. They all looked up as they heard the sound of a diesel motor stop, then a door close and finally footsteps coming up the driveway and around to the back gate.

"Evening, Leah." Ben called as the gate opened. "You're running late tonight with the truck."

Leah snorted as she came around to the deck. "It's been that kind of day, Ben. One of those days I wish I had never seen the sun come up."

Ben's keen eyes studied Leah. He could see the fatigue in her face and in the way she was moving. He mentally shook his head. What was Smitty thinking to let her run a tow truck?

"That bad, was it?" Then he took a closer look. She had her coveralls tied off at her waist and they were muddy and torn. A bandage covered a large portion of her left forearm as well as there being bruising on the arm and on her face. "What did you do?"

Leah looked up, a stormy look in her dark hazel eyes. "It's not what I did, Ben. It's what that idiot did." She stopped speaking as she realized they weren't alone. "I'm sorry, Ben. I didn't realize you had company. I just wanted to drop off the parcel Rory brought in for Marg."

"No problem, I don't think, Leah. Just a couple of fellows from my Bible study group. I don't think you've met them, have you?"

She shook her head. "No, I don't think I have."

"That young fellow over there is Ian Galbraith. You know Lydia Carmichael, they're engaged. This other young fellow is Joseph Broderick."

Greetings said, Leah went to move past her uncle, until he stopped her with a hand on her arm. "I heard what happened today, Leah. I spoke with Eddie. He's under review now."

Leah stared ahead, a closed look on her face. Joseph studied her intently and saw the dark look, almost a look of fear, that flitted through her eyes.

"That's great, Ben. Real great. When I disappear someday, then you'll know who to go after." She broke his contact with her and moved into the house.

Ben stared after her, then turned back to the two younger men, a thoughtful look on his face.

"Care to explain, Ben, or is it something you can't?" Ian's voice was quiet.

Ben's head turned to watch the back door, then he looked back at the two younger men.

"She drives a tow truck for her father. Today, she was hitching up a tow when an off-duty court officer ran her down or did his best to. If she hadn't hit the ditch, she would have likely been seriously injured, if not killed."

Joseph and Ian exchanged glances, a hard look coming onto their faces. Then Joseph spoke. "I hope he's been charged."

"Eddie says he has been. He's on paid leave for now, and that worries me."

Joseph watched the back door, waiting for Leah to come back out. "What's the deal, then, Ben? There has to be something."

"We can't figure it out. Leah doesn't like him, never has. She avoids him as much as she can."

Leah appeared at that moment. "I'm off for home, Ben." She lifted a foil-wrapped plate. "Marg's fed me."

Ben rose to his feet, drawing Leah into a hug. "Call me later. If you don't, I'll call you. Be careful."

"I intend to be. By the way, that move cost the city a tow contract. Dad's pulled us out." She sighed as her phone rang and she pulled it out.

"Smitty's. Leah speaking." Her face paling, she handed the phone to Ben, who listened, grim lines growing on his face.

"Davies, this is Ben Johnson. Just so you know, this will be reported." Ben listened to more words spewing across the air waves. "No, you're not going to do anything. You're off the force, and pretty much a civilian now. It's a different ball game for you. So back off." He clicked off her phone and handed it back to her. He studied her. "Be very careful, Leah. He'll be watching for you."

She sighed. "I know. Dad's already pulled me off tows. And that's not fair to women who appreciate having a female tow driver." She walked down the steps, then turned and glanced up at Ben. "I'll need your prayers, Ben, yours and Marg. My gut tells me it's only going to get a lot worse than it already is. You know some of the history. How do I stay safe from someone who has a history of violence like he does? And tell me, how did he get on the force in the first place and manage to stay there?" She turned and walked away, her footsteps heavy with fatigue.

She didn't see the car that pulled away from the curb and followed her, Davies throwing speculative glances at the house she had just left. So, he thought, she went running to her uncle. I'll deal with all of them soon.

Marg called them in for their meal at that point. As they sat and talked, the incident with Leah was uppermost in Joseph's mind. Lord, I just met this lady. Keep her safe.

Ben watched Joseph's face and nodded to himself. He's seen something in her, Lord, that most people miss. Is he the one who's going to be able to keep her safe from this trouble she's found herself in? Somehow, it's more than just what's going on with Davies and his conduct today. He's into something illegal and we need to find out what.

"Okay, Ben, so what's the deal with Leah? Or am I stepping into something that's none of my business?" Ian expressed

Joseph's thoughts, asking his question once again.

Ben and Marg exchanged a glance, then Marg spoke. "I don't think Ben's even aware of how deep this goes. Leah's talked to me in confidence. Not even her parents are aware of what she's told me." She paused to get her emotions under control. "Davies and Leah went to school together. For some reason, he's been fixated on her all her life, even though she's told him to stay away from her, her parents have told him, Caleb's told him. She has a restraining order out against him. He shouldn't have been anywhere near her today." Marg stopped again and turned her eyes to her husband.

"I never knew about the restraining order, Marg. When did she get that?"

"Last year. She said it was something similar to today. Only today was a lot worse. She saw him coming and jumped for the ditch. If she hadn't, she wouldn't be here."

Joseph and Ian exchanged glances, grimness in their looks. They knew better than even Ben the danger Leah now found herself in. Their employer trained security teams, but before Abe Finlay had switched to that, they had been one of the elite security teams in the country, sought after for their expertise.

"Does she have a boyfriend?" Ian's question caught both Ben and Marg off guard.

"No, she doesn't. She's dated in the past, but nothing for any length of time." Ben's eyes were on Marg and he saw the instant that she realized something. "You can't apply, Ian. You're engaged. Joseph, how about you?"

Joseph looked at Ben in surprise, then understood what he was asking. "That's an interesting thought, Ben. You want to talk to her?"

Laughter spilled into the room, and talk moved on to new topics.

Later as Ian drove them towards the security company grounds they called home, he spoke. "That situation with Marg's niece bothers me."

"I know, Ian. To think he acted like that, as a sworn officer of the law, and with a restraining order against him. I don't envy Caleb having to deal with him." Joseph stared out the side window of the truck, a thoughtful look on his face, missing the speculative glance Ian sent his way.

This is interesting, Lord. Joseph is always concerned about women and children's safety, but I don't think I've seen a look like that on his face. I wonder where it will go.

"Does Abe know her family?" Joseph question broke through the silence in the truck.

"I would imagine he does. Smitty's has been around for a while and is quite well known, I'm told. The company does local deliveries as well as tows." Ian eyed Joseph, waiting for a response. When none came, he spoke again. "Are you thinking of asking Abe to talk to her father?"

Joseph shrugged. "Not likely. If I did, I would be stepping in where I shouldn't."

Chapter 2

Leah sighed as she pulled her delivery van up to the gate at the factory complex. This is not what she wanted to be doing today. Lord, I just can't do this anymore, she thought. I need a change and I don't know what that change should be. I miss the tows. I miss helping those people. You've put me here on this route for now. Help me to be content.

"Hey, George. How are you today?" Her greeting floated across the small distance between the van and the guard house.

George peered out his window. "Leah! You're not Jones!"

Leah started to laugh. "I should hope not, George. Got my clearance? I won't be long today." She looked past him at the younger man standing beside him, dressed in a dark blue polo shirt with Rebel's embroidered on the left chest, eyes intent on her.

"I do, Leah. We're upgrading our security, so you'll need this new one."

"Thanks, George. For now, it will be either Dad, Rory or I making the deliveries."

George took another look at her, noting the bruising still evident on her face. "What happened to Jones?"

Leah started to laugh again. "It's not funny, I know, but he zigged when he should have zagged playing ball with his kids."

"Which one tripped him up?"

"The dog and he ended up breaking his arm. He's off for a while."

"That'll be some long hours for you three." George eyed her intently. "What about the tow company?"

"We're doing what we can there. We've found a couple of fellows to help out there. We're not doing the city contract now, so that helps."

"I heard what happened, Leah. Don't let me catch him."

She smiled at him. "Thanks, George. He's certainly put a price on his head, hasn't he?" With a wave, she drove off towards the factory receiving area.

George Walsh turned to the man who had stood silent the whole time. Micah, one of the Rebel's Security team and their computer expert, was working with George that day on the upgrades being put through.

"She's Smitty's daughter, and one of his drivers. She usually works on tows but I'm sure you've heard what happened." At Micah's nod, George sighed. "It shouldn't have happened, you know, it just shouldn't have happened."

Micah turned to watch the van moving away. Is this the lady that Ian told me about, who had caught Joseph's attention? "Ian mentioned something about it. She hasn't had any more run-ins with him that you know of, has she?"

George shook his head. "Not that I've heard. He'd be a fool to try anything more. But then, he's never had a real good grasp on what it means to be part of the community. I'm surprised he even made it on the force."

Micah nodded, then turned the conversation back to the security upgrade. But in the back of his mind, George's words echoed.

Leah backed her van into the designated spot and sat for a minute, her thoughts miles away. Maybe I just need to get away for a while. I haven't taken a vacation in a long time. Then she shook her head. No, that wasn't what was the matter with her. She could feel gathering storm clouds around her and a sense of evil. She didn't like it one bit. She grabbed her hand scanner and headed for the back of the van and her delivery.

She swiped her card in the lock and pulled the door open, pushing the hand cart in front of her. She quickly dumped her load in the receiving area, scanned the labels and headed for the office door.

She tapped at the open door, then stood in the doorway.

"Hey, Tweeter, need your signature." Her friend looked up from the paperwork he was studying.

"Leah. You're here. Where's Jones?" Tom Bell, or Tweeter as he was affectionately known as, was a good friend of hers from high school.

Leah shook her head. "He's off on sick leave for a while, Tweeter. Here, sign for your packages."

He signed, then stood and walked back through the receiving area with her. She could see other men moving around, ones she didn't know.

"What's going on, Tweeter?" Her voice was low.

"Security upgrades, Leah. That's all I can say." Tweeter's eyes were moving around the area, looking for what, he wasn't sure of. "We're have some incidents that we need to follow up on."

She nodded, then her eyes narrowed. "It must be some upgrade when you have Abe's company working it."

Tweeter shook his head. "You're too smart, Leah. Forget you saw anything, okay?" His voice had been low as they spoke. Then in a normal tone of voice, he asked, "If Jones is off, who'll be doing his runs?"

"Dad, Rory and I." Leah yawned. "I'm not sure about the early mornings. I liked my tow shift better."

"I know you did. You'll be back out there soon."

"I wish I had your confidence, Tweeter. Catch you later."

Joseph stood behind them, listening to their conversation. Tweeter had been careful in what he said, and Leah had been careful in what she asked. Interesting conversation,

Joseph thought, as he walked forward and stopped beside Tweeter.

"I didn't know Leah did deliveries."

Tweeter turned to him, catching a look on his face that stopped his words. He shot a look at the door that had closed behind Leah and then back at Joseph. What was up here, he wondered?

"Her Dad has a delivery service as well as a tow company. Leah works both, but she prefers working in the tow company."

Joseph shook his head. "It's not safe for her out there doing that." He turned and walked away, back to where Abe was working.

Tweeter stared after him, a puzzled look on his face. Well, Lord, that was an interesting conversation. Where's it leading to?

"I think this is going to work, Joseph. You've done good planning on this." Abe turned as Joseph approached him. His eyes narrowed at the slightly distracted look on Joseph's face and then traced past him. "Joseph, what's going on?"

Joseph mentally shook his head. "Nothing, Abe. Just that Leah MacGown was in with a delivery. When I see the

22

bruises on her face, it really makes me mad that someone tried to kill her."

Abe straightened up from where he had been crouched down, studying the security set up. He knew Leah, had been a classmate of hers, and she was a good friend of his sister, Rebecca. "What are you talking about?"

Joseph looked at him. "You haven't heard? She was almost run down yesterday by an off-duty court official."

"Davies." Joseph's eyes shot to Abe's face, and Abe nodded. "He's had it in for her for years. As well as a lot of other ladies in this town. Thankfully, Rebecca never got on his radar."

Joseph nodded, then turned his thoughts to what they were working on. In the back of his mind, he kept seeing her face, though. There is just something, Lord, about her that I can't forget. If it's in my ability to help her, let me.

Later that evening, Micah and Joseph stood outside of Mac's cafe, a favourite eating spot, waiting for Abe and Luke to catch up with them. The sound of a loud angry voice caught their attention across the parking lot

"That's Leah!" Joseph's exclamation and sudden move away from Micah startled him and then Micah was on his way after him.

Joseph didn't know the man standing in front of Leah in a threatening manner, arms waving with fists clenched. He approached Leah from behind, facing the man hurling venom and insults at her. Leah was frozen in place, a blank look on her face. Joseph reached gently and moved her behind him, confronting the man.

"I don't know what your problem is, but back off, buddy." Joseph seemed to tower over the man.

"Get out of here. This is none of your business." The man drew back a fist, ready to land it on Joseph, but Micah grasped his hand, preventing it

"Get her out of her, Joseph." Micah's words were quietly spoken. "Abe and Luke are behind you, and I can see a cruiser coming now."

Joseph nodded, then arm around Leah, led her to his truck and tucked her away inside. He stood, back against the open door, in a manner that he could keep his eye on Micah but also on Leah. She was white, a frightened look in her eyes. She was shivering, and Joseph reached for the blanket he kept in the back seat, wrapping it around her. As he finished, her hand came out to grasp his.

"Please don't let him hurt me again." Her words were barely audible.

Joseph shot a quick glance at the man now surrounded, then back at Leah.

"Leah." He waited for her to speak. "Leah. Is that Davies?"

She finally raised her face to him and nodded. "It is. I don't know where he came from tonight, but he was in front of me and I couldn't get away from him." Tears shimmered in the light. "Please, take me away from here."

Joseph nodded. "I will, Leah. In case you don't remember, we met at your uncle's the other night. I'm Joseph."

After a moment, she nodded. "I remember."

"Frankie's headed over here, Leah. Once you've spoken with him, I'll take you wherever you want. You can trust me."

Frankie stopped as he heard Joseph's words, a puzzled look on his face. When had Joseph met Leah, he wondered?

"Joseph?"

Joseph turned at the question in Frankie's voice and moved towards him.

"Frankie, what's up with that guy?"

Frankie shook his head. "I really don't know. Did he touch her tonight?"

"I don't know. Micah and I heard the confrontation and went to help." Joseph turned to look back at his truck. "She terrified, Frankie. It's beyond being scared. What has he done to her?"

"That's what we're trying to figure out. As far as we can determine, it's mostly words, one attempted hit and run a year ago and now this incident a few days ago. He's always been a bully. To tell you the truth, I don't know how he ever got to work in the courts." He stepped forward, so he could see Leah better. "I see what you mean, Joseph. She's been in some pretty dicey situations with her tows and is known for being fearless when she's helping someone. Quite often, she's the one the other tow companies will call on to help out stranded female motorists. I've never seen her like this."

"I don't know her at all, other than meeting her at Ben's, but I can tell you, I've seen this before. She's not scared, Frankie. She fears for her life. So, what do we do?"

Frankie nodded. "Let me speak with her. Then I suggest you get her out of here. Where does she want to go, her parents?"

"We hadn't got that far when you came over, but somehow, I don't think so. She's acting like someone who has had family and friends threatened. I've seen it in the past, Frankie. I know that look only too well."

Frankie shot him a look. That's the first I've ever heard Joseph say anything like that. I wonder what happened in his past.

"Leah!" Frankie spoke her name quietly, but she still jumped, eyes flying to him.

"Frankie, keep him away from me. Don't let him hurt me again!"

Frankie eyed her. He had never seen her like this, and she was one of his and Deirdre's friends. He spun to study the man now handcuffed and being pushed into the back of a cruiser. What have I walked into, Lord?

He turned back to the woman sitting in Joseph's truck. "Leah, what happened tonight?"

She shook her head, the shudders shaking her body becoming worse. "Keep him away from me, Frankie, please."

Abe approached as Frankie stepped away from the truck. He eyed Joseph, dipped his head to take a look at Leah, then turned to Frankie.

"Frankie, what's going on? Joseph told me today that Davies tried to run Leah down the other day. Now he confronts her like this?"

Frankie shook his head. "I don't know, Abe. That's what I need to talk to him about. He does have a restraining order against him and this won't be taken lightly, I can tell you that." He paused, eyes watching the cruisers pull away. "She's terrified, Abe. I have never seen anyone so terrified, and I've seen people scared before."

Abe nodded. "That's not her. So where do we take her?"

Chapter 3

Watching Frankie walk away, Joseph stood deep in thought, not seeing how Abe studied him.

"Joseph, where are you going to take Leah?"

Joseph shook his head to bring himself back to the present and turned to his friend. "I don't know, Abe. I'm not sure where she'll want to be. She's likely safe at home tonight, but she'll have to make long-term plans. This isn't over, not by a long shot."

Abe hesitated before he spoke, not wanting to tread on Joseph's privacy. "You've seen something like this before, Joseph, haven't you?"

Joseph nodded. "My sister. Only it didn't turn out the way we hoped." He stopped, lost in the past, eyes shadowed. "She never said anything until she had been beaten severely. She had been stalked every day. Every once in a while, I'd catch a similar look on her face to what's on Leah's. The police charged a former boyfriend, but he got out and came after her again." Joseph had to stop, emotions overcoming him. "They didn't find her body until two years later. By that time, he had committed suicide." He turned his eyes to Abe. "She covered it up so well, no one knew. Not even her closest friends. Not her family."

Abe's hand came down on Joseph's shoulder. "Thank you for telling me, Joseph." Abe hesitated before speaking. "We can use your help with Leah. I'm not sure she'll go to her parents or to Rory, or even Ben for that matter." He turned back to watch Leah. "Again, where are you going to take her for tonight?"

Joseph shrugged. "I don't know, Abe. All I was thinking about was getting her away from him and keeping her safe for the moment. I'm not sure she'll even be able to tell us where she wants to go."

"Let me talk to her. I might be able to get her to say." Abe turned back to the truck and stopped. "Joseph, did your sister ever act like Leah is?"

Joseph shook his head, then realizing Abe's back was to him, spoke. "No, she never did. She covered her fear only too well. Leah's a different personality that Ella was."

Abe wondered at what Joseph had said. As far as he knew, Joseph had only met Leah once, from what he had been told tonight. Yet, he read her so well. That was interesting, Lord. What's up with that? So far, Lord, You've matched my guys up so well with their ladies. Is this one Joseph's?

"Leah."

Abe's voice caught her attention and she turned to watch him. Joseph could see that the shuddering had stopped but she still kept herself wrapped in the blanket.

"Abe. Hi. Where did you come from?"

"I was to have supper here tonight, but a friend needed my help instead." He leaned against the side of the truck, eyes staring ahead. "Want to talk about it?"

She shook her head. "Not tonight. Knowing Frankie, I'll just have to go through it all again tomorrow. Thank you."

Abe shrugged. "I didn't do anything. Joseph here is the one who walked you away from that. Micah kept Davies from following you."

She shuddered at the name. Then her eyes sought Joseph. "Thank you. I appreciate what you did tonight. He usually doesn't let anyone walk away from him."

Joseph nodded. "He didn't have much choice, Leah. There was no way Micah was letting go of his hand and I wouldn't have let him touch you." He tilted his head to study her face, seeing the strain in it. "Tell us, what are you going to do for tonight? He'll not be out tonight."

She stared out the windshield of the truck. "He'll be out before I know it. I just wish I could leave and not come back here. It's been too many years of dealing with him and his friends."

Joseph stilled. "What do you mean, his friends?"

Leah sighed, then turned tired eyes towards them. "He has friends who threaten just like he does. Abe, talk to any of the females that were in our class. Even the married ones had trouble with him before they got married. Once they married, he backed off. Rebecca was always safe. He knew he couldn't mess with you or your Dad or uncle."

Abe started to speak, then stopped, his eyes studying Joseph, then turning to Micah and Luke. "How long has this been going on, Leah?"

She shrugged. "Since high school, I guess. He's a bully, Abe," she repeated. "He and all his friends are. Now, he has friends from outside of town, and I don't know who they are, so I can be careful. He's escalating in his violence. He's always hidden it, but it's there." She stopped, thinking of what had happened that night. "Abe, he's involved with the criminal element in town. Your guys will need to be careful now. He'll be after you."

Abe shrugged. "Won't be the first time. It's you we need to take care of tonight. Where do you want Joseph to take you?" He stopped and looked around the parking lot. "Where's your car?"

"At home. I walked."

Joseph stared at her. "How far away do you live?"

"A couple of miles, I guess. I needed the fresh air and the exercise."

"From now on, no walking anywhere." Joseph's face echoed the look on the other men's. "You've got an enemy here, Leah. You need to take precautions."

Leah glared at him, then was out of the truck, pushing past them to disappear in the darkness.

Joseph stared after her, then at Abe. "Did she really just do that?"

Abe nodded with a half-smile on his face. "She did. That's what she does. She's too determined to stand on her own two feet." He turned to stare around the parking lot.

Joseph stared in the direction Leah had walked off towards. "Any chance we can find her?"

Abe shrugged. "Maybe, but not likely. Why don't you and Micah take a drive by her house and wait for her? Here's the address. But I guarantee, she won't be happy to see you."

Joseph nodded. "I don't imagine she will be." As he turned, Abe laid his hand on his arm.

"Joseph, I'm sorry about your sister."

Joseph stopped, then looked at Abe, his eyes shuttered. "Thank you, Abe. She was more than just a sister; she was my twin." With that he walked around to the driver's side of his truck and climbed in, Micah seating himself in the passenger side.

Luke stared after the truck as Joseph drove away, shock at Joseph's admission coursing through him. "I never knew about his sister. Did you?"

Abe shook his head. "You guys are so quiet about your lives, it's always a surprise when something comes out. Let's head for home, Luke. I don't have an appetite any more for food."

Luke agreed, his thoughts moving through what had happened, and what he knew would come. Lord, he prayed, keep Leah safe, and protect our Joseph's heart.

Chapter 4

Frankie looked up from his desk as he heard his name called. Abe stood in his doorway, hesitating about entering.

Frankie frowned, then motioned him in. "Abe, what can I do for you?" He watched as his friend sat, not saying anything.

"Frankie, about last night. What's going on?"

Frankie sat back. He had expected one of Abe's fellows to be in but he expected it to be Joseph, not Abe. "What do you mean? About Leah?"

Abe nodded. "She said something after you left that really disturbed me. Did you know Davies at all when we were in school?"

Frankie shook his head. "I'd see him around the school but didn't have contact with him outside of any shared classes. He always ran with a rough crowd. What did she say that has you so disturbed?"

"She said that he's involved in the criminal element in town. She also said that every female in our class had had problems with him. Did they ever say anything?"

Frankie shook his head. "Not that I'm aware of. I wish one of them had. Then maybe we wouldn't be sitting here having this conversation."

Abe agreed. He stood. "Joseph and Micah will be in today to sign their statements. I just wish..." His voice trailed off as he walked away.

What do you wish for, Abe? The same thing I do, that Davies had never been in this town? He's created a whole lot of paperwork and trouble. Frankie sighed as he looked down at some of that paperwork on his desk. I just had to be the one, didn't I, Lord, that got that call. I want to help Leah, but I have no idea how.

Leah turned from the windows in her father's office, a frown on her face and fire in her eyes. "I'm not quitting driving, Dad. I refuse to grant him that much control over my life. He's had enough."

Smitty sat and watched his daughter. "How do we keep you safe then, Leah?"

"It won't matter if I'm out on my own business or company business. He finds me every time. I just can't shake him." She watched her father's face and saw the distress there. "I couldn't tell you, Dad. He threatened each one of you, including Marg and Ben."

"By keeping quiet, honey, you allowed him to continue to terrorize you." Smitty held up his hand. "I hear what you're saying and why you did what you did. But now, we need to come to some sort of understanding of what we do now. Frankie's talked to me about last night. He knew you wouldn't have." He paused. "So, who was this young man who stepped in?"

Leah shrugged as she sat down. "He's in Ben's Bible study group and I met him when I dropped off that parcel for Marg. They just happened to be there in the parking lot last night."

Smitty grinned. "Just happened to be, did he?" Leah shook her head at her father as he continued. "No just happened about it. God put him there. You say he works for Abe? Then, we'll have a talk with Abe and see what he can suggest." At her protest, he shook his head again. "No, Leah, we're going to do what we need to for your safety. What that is yet, I don't know."

"Fill me in when you and Abe come up with a plan, and I'll let you know if I'm going to go along with it. Catch you later."

Smitty watched as his daughter walked out of the room, heading for her delivery van, he knew. *Did I do wrong, Lord, in letting her work for me like this?* He turned back to his paperwork, but it was a while before he picked up his pen, only to lay it down again. He searched his phone for a number and then made a call. He was setting in works a plan he hoped would keep his daughter safe but no one could guarantee it.

Joseph turned from the security plans he was working on for a new client and stared out the window near his desk. *What was going on with Leah,* he wondered? He had to tamp down the anger he felt towards Davies. Davies was the type of man Joseph despised, a man who was everything Joseph was not. He didn't want to see anyone else go through what Ella had. Leah was too nice a person to have that happen to. He smiled to himself. No, that wasn't it all. She was beautiful, and he liked what he had seen so far. He wanted to get to know her better, but circumstances certainly weren't right for that.

Abe looked up from the schedule planning he was working on and watched Joseph. Smitty's phone call had come out of the blue, but he should have expected it, he knew. What Smitty had asked would be difficult to manage, but somehow Abe planned to provide men to watch Leah as much as he could. His thoughts turned to what Joseph had shared the night before. He nodded. Joseph was the one they needed with Leah. Now, how to arrange that.

He stood and wandered over to where Joseph had gone back to work.

"How are the plans coming together?"

Joseph looked up, blinking as his concentration was broken. "Good, I think, Abe. He's a reasonable client to work with, willing to do what he needs to." Joseph sat back in his chair, staring at the monitor. "It just seems strange that we have so many new clients wanting security upgrades. More than we've ever had at one time."

Abe perched on the corner of the desk. "I know. I've been trying to figure that one out as well. It's not just the big companies, either."

Joseph shook his head. "No. We're get more smaller companies than we did." He hesitated, then looked through folders on his desk. "I had Micah run a demographic search on the companies. I was going to go over this with you this afternoon. I don't like what I'm seeing."

Abe took the folder and opened it. "I have to agree, Joseph. There's a pattern there, isn't there?" He stared at the paperwork, then looked up. "Any thoughts?"

Joseph shook his head. "I'm still trying to work through the companies and what they handle. There seems to be a wide range of companies, but what their commodities are can be dealt quickly on the black market. I'm just afraid someone's going to be in the wrong place at the wrong time."

Abe agreed. "That would be my fear, too. We don't have enough to warn anyone either." He closed the folder and dropped it back on Joseph desk, trying in his mind now to find the words to broach the subject he needed to. "Smitty called me this morning."

"Is Leah okay?" Joseph's eyes flew to Abe's.

So, that's how it is, Abe thought. About what I figured. "She is. She's not happy with her father though for trying to come up with a way to keep her safe."

Joseph sat back once again in his chair, eyes narrowing as he watched Abe. "And why do I feel like Nathaniel right about now?"

Abe started to laugh. Nathaniel had played the part of Elizabeth's boyfriend when they needed to keep her safe, but the two had ended up falling in love and were planning a wedding in the near future. "Are you saying you're willing to be the one taking care of her?"

Joseph sat forward, leaning his arms on the desk top. "That's a good question, Abe. There is no way I would do anything like that without her full cooperation. That's not who I am. And we can't spring it on her like you did with Elizabeth."

"No, we can't. She couldn't handle that." Abe paused, then spoke again. "Joseph, knowing what you went through with your sister, can you suggest ways we can keep Leah safe, other than sticking her in a room somewhere and throwing away the key?"

Joseph laughed at that vision. "That definitely won't work. She's already chafing at not driving tows, from what Micah overheard yesterday. I'll think about it and see what I can come up with."

Abe stood to go back to his desk. "Now, if you just happened to be around her home when she got off work and asked her to dinner at Mac's, think she would go?"

Joseph shook his head. That was exactly what he wanted to do, and he knew he shouldn't.

Caleb Logan, Police Chief, looked up as Frankie knocked at his door and then entered.

"You look like you really don't want to be here," Caleb remarked.

"I don't. We had another incident with Davies last night. He's terrorized Leah. Joseph and Micah just happened to be there when the incident went down." Frankie brought Caleb up to date on what had happened.

"Davies has always been a loose cannon. I know Hannah never liked him when we were at school with him. Sounds like he's gotten even worse."

"That's what I'm hearing, Caleb. Why didn't the guys know about this?"

Caleb shrugged. "Who know? Guess we were too busy living life to notice what was going on. What does Leah want to do now?"

Frankie shook his head. "I still have to talk to her again this morning, then go back to talk with Joseph and Micah." He stood. "I don't like it, Caleb. My gut says something else is going on, and Leah has somehow found herself in the midst of it."

Caleb studied his friend. "Not another one. Keep me updated and let me know what I can do to help."

Micah approached Abe later that day, Joseph at his side. "Abe, I think we have a real problem."

Abe turned, surprised at the grim tone in Micah's voice. "What is it?"

"Those companies that are upgrading their security systems? Smitty's does a lot of deliveries to them." He handed Abe the folder he had in his hand. "I've expanded the search Joseph asked me to do, and this is what I came up with."

Abe shot him a quick glance, then opened the folder. "All of them?"

Joseph nodded. "It smells like a set-up to me. You'll need to talk to Smitty."

"I agree. Micah, you're with me. Joseph, go find Leah and stick with her. Smitty said she should be done her run about this time and be at home."

Chapter 5

Leah was tired. The day had been long, and the strain of her talk with her father that morning still weighed heavy on her. She wanted nothing more than to crash on her couch and just do nothing, but she had things she needed to do. As she pulled into her driveway, a truck parked at the curb caught her attention. Please, Lord, don't let it be Davies or one of his cronies. I just can't do this anymore. I used to feel safe and secure at my home and now I don't.

As she walked towards her front door, a voice called her name. She turned, surprised. What was Joseph doing here?

"Leah. Hi." Joseph stopped at the bottom of the stairs and watched her. She's tired, he thought, tired and worn out. We need to do something to lift that burden she's been carrying.

"Joseph. What are you doing here? Did you decide to come on your own or did

Dad put you up to it?" Leah's tone was cutting, her frustration evident.

Joseph held up a hand. "Back off, Leah. I'm here on my own. Your dad didn't ask me to come. I was concerned after last night and wanted to make sure you were okay. Abe's concerned about his friend as well."

"And you couldn't have just called?" She continued to unlock her door and silence her security system. She turned and sighed. "You may as well come in."

Joseph stood just inside the closed front door. "No one asked me to come. I had the bright idea to come see you all by myself. I guess I shouldn't have." He turned, hand on the knob when her voice stopped him.

"Joseph, I'm sorry. It's been a rough week, but that's no excuse for taking it out on you."

He heard her boots hit the boot tray as he turned. "I know it has been. How about you come out to get something to eat with me?"

"Why?"

"Why what?" Joseph knew what she was asking but wanted to see what her response would be.

"Why me, Joseph? If it's pity, there's the door. I don't do pity."

"I didn't think you did. No. I want to spend some time with you. Is that a crime? If so, tell me and I'll leave."

She studied him, taking in the dark blue eyes and the dark blond hair. "Where?"

"Where? I don't care. You can pick. Or if you prefer, we can order in."

She shook her head. "I'll need a few minutes to change. I'm grubby from work."

He nodded as he opened the door. "I have a book. Take your time."

She watched as the door closed, then turned to head for her bedroom. *Why now, Lord? Why bring someone into my life when it's such a mess?* Then her hands stilled as she brushed her short cap of brown curls. *Is he the one, Lord? Is he the one who will finally stop the terror I've been facing for so many years?* She closed her eyes and then sighed. *No, it would never happen that way.* She grabbed her purse and keys and headed for the door. *Tonight would be interesting,* she thought.

Joseph sat in thought, his book open on his knee, as he waited for Leah to reappear. *Lord, what is it about her that draws me? It's* more than the problem she was facing. There's just something about her that makes me want to get to know her better. I've never felt like that before. Then his eyes sought the neighbourhood around her home. He could feel the danger, the evil that threatened her. Now I know how the other guys felt. Lord, protect this lady. If it's in my ability to do so, use me. He turned as he heard the door open and then close again. Leah stood watching him, eyes questioning.

He stood and reached for her hand. "Come on, sweet lady. Where do you want to eat?"

She looked down at their hands, then back up at his face. His smile had reached his eyes. She smiled back.

"I have no idea. Just not Mac's, please."

"No problem. Do you have any preference?" He shut the door after her and then slid behind the wheel.

She shrugged, then shivered. "I don't like feeling like this, Joseph, feeling threatened all the time. I feel him all around him all the time."

Joseph nodded. "I can feel it too. I'll do my best to keep you safe. That's a promise I intend to keep."

She nodded. "Somehow, Joseph, I know you'll try but I don't think anyone can keep a promise like that." She drew a deep breath. "So, where are we headed for supper or dinner or whatever you want to call it?"

The forced enthusiasm for a meal tugged at his heart. "I have no idea what you like to eat."

"Italian. Fish and chips. I really don't have a preference other than I'm not crazy about Chinese food."

Joseph smiled as his eyes caught the lights in his mirror. He had a tail. Now he had to shake it. "How about Italian, then?"

She turned to him, then caught his quick look in his mirrors. "Is someone following us?"

He shrugged. "With my line of work, I'm always extra cautious. Nothing to worry about."

She snorted. "Yeah, right."

Later, as he walked her to her door, he searched the area once again. He could still feel him, whoever it was. "Busy day for you tomorrow?" he asked.

She shook her head. "I'm off tomorrow and plan to leave town for the day."

"By yourself?" He looked down at her.

"Of course, by myself. I just need some time away."

Joseph stood as she unlocked her door and bit his lip, hesitating to say something. She looked up at him, saw the hesitation on his face, and tilted her head.

"What are you not sure about, Joseph?"

"I would like to spend more time with you." He looked up and stared down the hall in her house. "I just happen to have tomorrow off. Our team isn't doing any training until next week."

She started to laugh. "And you don't know how to ask if you can come and tag along with me tomorrow?" She shook her head. "Joseph, you don't strike me as someone who would hesitate this way."

He shook his head. "With you, I'm not sure how to ask anything. So, can I?"

She laughed again at him. "Yes, you may. I had planned to leave early and spend the day far away from here"

He nodded, as he reached a hand up to touch her cheek. "Good night, then. Lock up when you go in. I'll wait."

"Good night, Joseph." She stood leaning back against the door after she had locked it, lost in thought. She finally shook her head and walked down the hall. She had some things she just had to get done tonight if she was spending tomorrow away from here.

Abe watched as Joseph drove away the next morning, looking at his watch. He's away early this morning, Lord. I have a bad feeling, though, keep his safe.

Later that morning, Abe looked up from his paperwork when a knock came to the office door and both Frankie and Abe's uncle and police detective, Eddie Brown, entered. His eyes narrowing, he watched as they sat, looked at each other and then at him.

"This isn't a social call, I can tell. Spit it out."

Eddie looked at his nephew. "Where's Joseph?"

Surprise, Abe shrugged. "He took off early this morning. The team isn't working until next week, so they're up to whatever they want to be." He looked between the two men. "Again, what's up? Something is to bring you out here together and with those looks on your faces."

Frankie pulled his phone out and pulled up a text message. "Someone sent me this text this morning."

Abe reached for it, hesitation in his movements. "That bad?"

"Just take a look at it, Abe. Then, we need to talk." Eddie watched Abe's face as he read the text.

Chapter 6

Abe stilled as he looked at the picture, then read the text.

"This isn't aimed at Leah, is it?" His eyes raised, his question more of a statement.

Frankie shook his head. "No, it's directed at you, Abe. We need to find out who and why."

"We've been through this before. I have no clue who it could be."

Abe read the message again.

"Your time is coming, Finlay. How many of your men have to be hurt?"

He looked at the picture attached. "That picture has to be from today."

Eddie agreed. "We talked to Smitty. Leah had the day off today. They haven't been able to reach her, but he says if she's off for the day, she generally mutes her phone and lets it go to voice mail."

Abe handed Frankie back his phone. "Here's Joseph's number. Forward that to him and warn him to be careful." Abe sat back in his chair, his mind spinning, going over the incidents in the past few months with his men. Nothing stuck out to him as to the culprit was. Why him?

Abe reached for Frankie's phone again. Something puzzled him about the picture. He studied it again.

"Joseph has seen something. I can tell by the way he's looking behind him. And he's getting Leah ready to move way."

Frankie and Eddie exchanged glances, then Frankie reached for his phone. "How can you tell?"

"I just know Joseph well enough to see that."

The office door opened at that moment and Micah stepped in, hesitating when he saw who was there.

"Micah, did Joseph happen to say what his plans were today?"

Abe's question caught Micah off guard. He shook his head. "I haven't talked to him since yesterday afternoon some time. Is there a problem?"

Abe nodded and motioned him over, showing him the text and picture. Micah's face set into stern lines, then he commented, "That's at the old factory stores in Greentown."

Eddie was on his feet and out the door, phone in hand, before Micah had completely finished. Frankie's eyes met Abe's and Abe nodded. Eddie was making a call to a friend on that force.

Joseph felt the tingling in his neck he always felt when he was in danger. Searching around him didn't show him who it was, but he knew he had to get Leah out of there as soon as he could. He reached for her hand and pulled her with him through the crowds.

"Joseph, what's going on?" Leah tugged at her hand, trying to free it.

Joseph's hand tightened even more. "We need to get out of here, Leah. Someone's watching one of us, and we need to disappear quickly."

She picked up her pace to keep even with him. "One of us? Are you sure?"

Joseph nodded as he shot a quick glance behind him. "Absolutely. I know that feeling only too well. It's part and parcel of my job."

She drew a deep breath. "Davies or one of his cronies?"

Joseph shook his head as he shot a glance behind him. "I don't know. Someone's there. I can still feel him somewhere near us."

"What about getting to your truck?"

Joseph shook his head. "It's too easy for them to get us there." He paused for a moment to catch his breath as they emerged from the crowds.

"There!" Leah pointed. "The old-fashioned, open streetcar's just about to leave. If we catch it, we can figure out what we need to do."

"Come on, then." Pulling her after him, he ran for the street car, lifting her up and swinging up behind her as it pulled away. Wrapping an arm around her, he stood so his back was towards the direction they had just come from and she was protected. He shot a glance behind him.

A short heavyset man emerged from the crowd and stopped, frustration in his bearing. It was him, Joseph thought. He pulled out his phone and snapped a quick picture. Maybe Micah can do something with it, he thought.

"What now, Joseph?" Leah was trying her best to act nonchalant, but Joseph could feel the tremors flowing through her.

"We get off in a couple of stops, find somewhere we can catch our breath, and make some plans."

Joseph's eyes were in constant motion. His security training had kicked in, and he was on watch. *Please, Lord, help me to keep Leah safe and secure. I don't know who or why, but You do. Guide our decisions and steps over the next few hours.*

As the streetcar slowed, Joseph dropped to the pavement, catching Leah as she followed him. Grasping her hand again, he pulled her towards a small cafe just around the corner, and then into it, finding a booth at the back. He shoved her onto one of the seats and then slid in beside her.

She took a look at him, then peered around him. "So, tell me, is this what your life is like? All this excitement and danger and foot chases?"

Joseph stared at her, then caught the glint of mischief in her eyes. He shook his head. "Not usually. Abe usually has everything and everyone under control. But lately it seems that when we're out and about, anything goes, especially if we're out with a lady."

She leaned back on the seat and stared at the other bench seat. "So now what?"

Joseph grabbed for a menu. "We need to keep up our cover. What do you want to eat?"

Her eyes flickered between him and the menu and then back. "Are you serious? Eating at a time like this?"

Joseph turned to her and spoke in a low voice. "Leah, trust me on this. We need to pretend we're just out for a meal until I can figure out how to get us back to my truck. No, that won't work. They'll be watching it, likely."

"Order me something. I don't care what." She pulled out her phone and scrolled through the contact list.

"I have a friend with a tow company here in town. If we can get him to tow your truck somewhere we can meet him. Then maybe we can get on our way."

"So how will that work? They'll follow him and the truck."

"I know, but if he takes it to his recycling yard, there's a back entrance only a few people know about. We can get out that way." She punched in his number.

"Dennis, Leah MacGowan. How are you? Good. The family? That's good. Listen, I need your help, or rather a friend and I do." She explained the situation to him, as much as she could. "You'll help?" Her eyes found Joseph's and she nodded. "Here's Joseph. It's his truck and he can give you the details you need. Give us about 30 minutes to get to your yard."

Joseph handed her back her phone when he was done. "Will this work?"

"I hope so." She looked at the plate of food in front of her. "I'm not hungry, you know."

"Try and eat something. It's going to be a long night, I think. I'm praying this works." He pulled out his phone and forwarded the picture to Micah. Then he saw the text from Frankie and pulled it up. His fingers stilled, and he could feel the fear for Leah's safety rushing through him.

Leah, looking up to say something, saw the look on his face, and hand on his, turned the phone so she could see it. "That's just when you pulled us out of there, isn't it?"

He nodded. "I could feel eyes on us, and a sense of evil. God got us from there and He'll get us home."

She looked up at him. "How can you be so confident in that, Joseph?"

He shrugged. "I guess because He's done it over and over with me and the team. How long will it take for us to get to your friend's?"

She shrugged. "Twenty minutes? It's not really that far from here."

"Okay, then we have time to finish our meal." Joseph stared into the distance, lost in thought, until Leah touched his hand.

"Joseph, come back from wherever it is you are."

He turned to her and studied her face. "Thank you for today, Leah."

She tilted her head and then shook it. "I don't get you, Joseph. Who raised you?"

He started laughing as he dropped money on the table for their meal and then pulled her to her feet. "My parents. Mom was very strict about politeness. Still is in fact." As they left the cafe, his eyes roamed the crowds. Who is there, Lord, that I can't see? "I need to take you to meet them one day soon."

Leah stopped in her tracks, her mouth dropping open, until Joseph pulled her forward with him. "Take me home to meet your parents? Joseph!"

He laughed at her, then drew her closer to him. "Which way, my lady, are we to head?"

Chapter 7

Joseph's steps slowed as they approached the recycling yard Leah had led them to. His eyes searching in the dim light, he finally stopped in the shadows and waited. Leah stood beside him, puzzled at his moves.
"Joseph?" Her voice had a question.

His fingers on her lips, he leaned close. "Don't talk. I want to make sure your friend wasn't followed. And he was."

Leah's eyes searched the darkness but couldn't see anything out of the ordinary. What had Joseph seen?

His mouth close to her ear, he whispered, "Where's this back entrance you talked about?"

She nodded and then led him back the way they had just come and around the yard to the back. She slipped through a portion of the wall, pulling him with her, then shoving the metal back into place. Beckoning him forward, she headed for the office, stopping just out of the light that was streaming from the window. Joseph could see his truck, nose towards the back of the yard, waiting for him. Leah finally moved towards the side of the building, away from the light, and feeling her way along the blocks, found the door she was looking forward. She slipped through it, followed by Joseph, then turned and locked it behind her.

"Have you done this before?" Joseph's question caused her to laugh.

"In my dreams, maybe. You're rubbing off on me, you know." She led the way forward, then stopped when she heard voices.

Joseph shoved her behind him and crept silently towards the open door. He listened, then urged her forward.

"Your friend seems to be by himself. Text him and make sure, okay?"

They could hear Dennis' phone chime and then it went silent. They waited, not sure what was happening. Leah's phone finally chimed quietly.

"You need to leave out the back. They're watching the front, whoever they are. Take care, Leah. Let me know how you are."

Then another text came through. "Wait. Denny Jr has a vehicle out back for you. Take it. Have your friend leave his keys and we'll get his truck back to him, even if we have to tow it."

Leah sent a quick text back. "Thanks, Dennis. I owe you."

"No, you don't. It's the other way around, the way I see it."

Once outside the yard, Joseph quietly shut the door to the old beat-up pickup truck and climbed behind the wheel.

"Will it run?" he asked Leah.

"If it's Denny Jr's, then it will. He is a wonder with these old vehicles."

Abe turned as Micah headed towards him and waited until he caught up to him.

"Joseph sent me a picture of a fellow he thinks was following him. I've traced it back to being a friend of Davies. That doesn't tie with the text Frankie received."

"That's just great. So he had two different lots after him today." Abe ran his hands through his hair in frustration. "So, where do we stand?"

"Right now, with that text of Frankie's, nowhere. Untraceable phone." Micah was visibly upset that he couldn't find any information. "I've tried everything I could. I even passed it on to Jace at Tracker's. He couldn't get anything either."

"Now, that's hard to believe. Jace is good." Abe turned to study the hill and rocks around the compound. "So now what?" He stopped as his phone chimed.

"It's Joseph, or at least I think it is. No, Leah. She says they're safe and on their way home. She also says Joseph will explain when he gets here." Abe looked up at Micah. "That's a strange text."

"It is." Micah reached for Abe's phone. "It's from his phone. Wonder what's up?"

Joseph watched as Leah sent the text to Abe, then reached for her own phone.

"It's Denny, Jr." She started laughing. "Take a look around us, Joseph. He's got us surrounded with his friends."

Lights popped up all around them. "How many are there?"

"He says a dozen and that two or three cruisers are waiting for us. He's left us jackets and caps to put on." She started laughing even harder. "He's been watching too many cop shows. He's got this plan to

65

get us out of here and it involves us driving right past the front of the yard.”

“The front of the yard, huh? Well, I guess it’s no more dangerous than what we’ve already been through.” Joseph stopped and reached for her hand. “Before we go anywhere, we need to pray. God has to be the one in charge.”

She nodded.

Abe turned as he heard an unfamiliar truck pull into their home area later that night. He walked towards it as Joseph stepped out.

“Joseph! You’re okay?”

Joseph nodded, then grinned. “Leah has quite the group of friends. This truck belongs to the son of one of her tow friends. He picked up my truck for me and then sent us on our way in this. He was followed by whoever it is that is either after me or after Leah.”

“Really? She certainly has some resourceful friends.”

“Her comment was that Denny, Jr., was watching too many cop shows. Speaking of which, we had an escort out of Greentown to town. Did you arrange that?”

“No, but I know Eddie was looking into finding you.”

Joseph shook his head, then yawned. "I'll catch up with you in the morning, Abe." He turned and headed for his cabin, fatigue in his steps.

Abe watched until the lights came on in the cabin, then turned to seek his own rest. A flash of light in the rocks stopped him. What was that? He made a mental note to take one of the team and search up there in the morning.

Leah turned from her phone and set it down by her bed. How sweet, she thought, Joseph's text to wish me good night. He's such an interesting man and so thoughtful. Wonder where this will lead?

Chapter 8

Smitty watched as his daughter crossed to her delivery van. He was sending her out with the smaller van and a shorter route today. Rory was taking over the longer one until their drivers were all back. She hadn't been happy about it, but he had put his foot down. He knew she'd come around to his way of thinking, eventually, maybe? These days, he just wasn't sure of how she would react. She hadn't said where she had been yesterday other than she had been out of town with a friend.

He turned as a knock came to his door, and it opened to reveal Abe and Joseph. What's up with these two being here so early, he wondered? Don't tell me something happened yesterday, his heart dropping. He walked towards them, hand out to shake theirs, then pointed to his office and the chairs there.

"Abe, for you to be here this early, it's not good, I take it."

"No, it's not, Smitty." Abe hesitated, not sure how to continue.

"The thing is, Smitty," Joseph spoke up, "Leah and I spent the day in Greentown. We were followed by someone connected to Davies. Her friend, Dennis, and his son helped us to elude them last night. But it concerns me that she is being followed like she is."

Smitty sank into his chair, eyes fixed on the two men in front of him. "You're sure?"

Joseph nodded. "I snapped a picture to send to Micah to see if he could track down who it was, and she recognized him. Davies is escalating what he's doing."

Smitty's head sank into his hands. "If only she had told me earlier, I could have dealt with it before it got to this point."

Abe shook his head. "I doubt that, Smitty. He's kept it pretty secret and quiet until now. For some reason, he's escalating in violence towards her." Abe and Joseph shared a look, then Abe spoke again. "Joseph's been working on setting up new security systems in a number of companies in the area. He noticed a trend and asked Micah to do some research. This is what we've found." He handed over the folder he had been carrying.

Smitty took it with a quick look at Joseph, then opened it to read. "All of these are on our route. What's the connection?"

"That's what Micah is looking into. There's something there, Smitty, and it looks like Davies and his cronies are up to something that will make you take a fall for them."

Smitty nodded. "I know a couple of them now have government contracts. About five already do. That's your connection, Abe. You need to find out what they're working on for the government. This is just new for all this companies. Somewhere, there's a leak that has led Davies and his friends to that. I can't think of anything else." He looked at Abe, then studied Joseph. "How do we keep Leah and Rory and the rest of my drivers safe?"

"That's what Joseph and I and the other team members have been discussing. Can you double up your drivers?"

Smitty shook his head. "No. I just have enough now to do the routes with one off sick. I've pulled Leah off the longer runs and put her on the small van. Rory's taken over the other run. To say she wasn't happy would be an understatement."

Joseph smiled, then said, "Do what you need to, Smitty, to ensure her safety. She was scared last night, but the other night when Davies confronted her, she was absolutely terrified."

"The other night?" Smitty's eyes bored into Joseph. "What are you talking about?"

Joseph sighed. "I guess she didn't tell you? Davies confronted her at Mac's. Abe, Luke, Micah and I were there. Micah contained Davies. But I can tell you, I have never seen someone so terrified. And before you go and tell her you know, you can't. That would break a thread of friendship I have with her, and we need that."

Smitty's eyes never left Joseph's face as he spoke. Then, he sighed. "I know you're right, but she's my little girl, and I want to make it all better for her."

"We understand that, Smitty, and we want to come up with a plan that will keep her safe." Abe looked at Joseph, catching a look on his face he had seen before. Here we go again, Lord. Protect Joseph and his lady. "We need to know exactly who your drivers are, their routes, and the companies you deliver to. That way, we can come up with a plan."

"I can do that. I'll have my secretary draw that up for me."

"Smitty, we don't want anyone to know what's going or why we need it."

Smitty stopped, hand on his phone, and stared at Abe, then at Joseph. He nodded. "I understand. We've been doing some work on something like that anyway, trying to divide up the work with a driver off. It shouldn't take May long to get that for me." After he had requested the information, he turned to Abe. "So, what are your thoughts on this?"

Abe studied him, then spoke. "I need to get together with Caleb for one and also Frankie and Eddie likely as there will need to be an investigation launched. We haven't gotten to that point yet, but it is coming. I'm sure they'll be speaking with you."

Smitty nodded. "I'm sure they will be. Tell them to call me when they are. I'll keep working on what I can. What about Leah? How do we keep her safe?" Smitty's voice cracked with worry about his daughter.

Abe shot another look at Joseph, hesitating, but before he could speak, Joseph did.

"Smitty, I spent yesterday with your daughter. She's a wonderful lady. I told her I would like to explore a friendship with her, and she has agreed. I don't know where God will lead this, but it is in His hands. I just want you to know that I will do everything possible to keep her safe when she's with me."

Smitty sat back and studied the young man sitting in front of him, assessing him. He liked what he saw in Joseph's face, knew Abe wouldn't have him on his team if he didn't trust him or know his character. "Tell you what, Joseph. You do just that." Then a spark of mischief lit his face, reminding the Joseph of the look on his daughter's face yesterday. "And when you decide you want to spend the rest of your life with her, come talk to me again."

Joseph clenched his jaw to keep it from dropping open, then reached to shake Smitty's hand as they stood. "I'll do that, Smitty."

Abe was laughing as he climbed behind the wheel of his SUV. "I think you just got found out, Joseph."

Joseph threw him a look and then shook his head. "Not you too. I never expected him to say that. Now, what are we to do with the information he's given us?"

"Get Micah working on it. And take a copy to Jace at Tracker's and see what he can come up with." Abe was thoughtful. "I think we need to go talk to Caleb. This is getting bigger than we expected, Joseph."

"And if it is the government contracts, then we have the government involved. But that doesn't feel right, Abe. I still think it's something else."

Abe nodded. "I agree. Making us think it's the government contracts is a smokescreen. Is Jace still digging?"

"Micah asked him to. He thought he'd have more for us today at some point."

"So, where do you go with Leah now, Joseph?"

Joseph shrugged. "I don't know, Abe. I really don't know. And before you say it, I know I'm facing an uphill battle just like the other guys did."

"Not as much as you think, Joseph. Leah's a strong personality, has decided opinions, but she is open to listening. Just not open to doing what you think she should. Smitty's as much as said that about her driving the van." Abe paused. "I've known her for so many years. She's friends with Rebecca. Talk to Rebel if you need to, to get a feel of how to approach Leah."

Joseph nodded, his thoughts drifting back to the day before. Abe had a read on Leah, but it wasn't the same as what Joseph had picked up. Leah had a deep-down fear of Davies and his friends and she had never shared that until now. Please, Lord, let me help her. Guide her to the security she can have in you. I can see she is struggling with her faith at this point. "I see her differently, Abe, maybe because I didn't grow up with her. She's more than scared and she's trying to figure out how to get away and protect her family at the same time."

Abe shot a glance at Joseph. Once again, he was amazed at the perceptions he could draw from when he met people. He had an ability to read people on first meeting that few Abe had met did. "What are you saying, Joseph?"

"Just that you don't know her as well as you think you do. Her parents don't either." Joseph sighed, his face becoming shadowed with sorrow. "It was like that with Ella. She was brilliant, bubbly, full of life, but hid such a dark secret. She didn't let us see the real Ella underneath."

Chapter 9

Leah took note of the truck parked once again in front of her home and smiled. Joseph was waiting for her. She could get used to this, she thought, then shook her head. Not likely. Davies would scare him away, just like every other boyfriend she had ever had.

Joseph looked up from where he had seated himself on her front steps and smiled. Leah wasn't as tired today, he thought.

"You're back!" Leah smiled as she stopped in front of him.

He stood. "I am. Care to go out for supper again?"

She shook her head. "Is this to be a nightly occurrence, us having dinner together?"

"I would like that, but it's your decision, Leah." Joseph watched her face as he spoke.

She studied him. *Please, Lord, let him be the one. Let him be the one who scares Davies and his friends away. I can't go on any longer under this shadow of terror I've been living under. It has tried so much of my life, including my walk with You.*

"You sound like a confident man there, Joseph."

"I try to be. So supper out or in?"

"Let me get cleaned up and we can decide. Come on in."

He shook his head. "No, I'll wait here again."

She looked at him, then nodded. "No problem. Give me about fifteen minutes or so. Where to tonight?"

"You can be thinking about that and let me know."

She shook her head. "The other night, we went where I chose. Tonight, it's your choice."

Joseph listened as the door closed behind him, then his eyes sought the street. He could feel the evil getting closer. *Where is he, Lord? Can we not just deal with it tonight and get it over with?* He felt the peace come over him that he always felt just before a security assignment took over the team. He knew that now was the time to fight, to protect his lady. His lady! He liked the sounds of that. If only she would be, Lord, if only.

Leah studied Joseph as she closed and locked her front door, then sat down on the steps beside him.

"Where did you decide we'd go, Joseph?"

He shrugged. "I don't really care, Leah. It's not the meal, it's who I'm with that matters."

"You really mean that, don't you?" At his nod, she looked up to the sky. "Where were you years ago, Joseph, when I needed someone in my life?"

"Right where God wanted me to be, Leah. The timing wasn't right years ago. We don't know why God has led you through what He has, but I do know He is there every step with you."

She nodded. "I just get so scared at times."

Joseph reached for her hand and pulled her to her feet. "I know you do. That's what I want to take away from you, that fear. I couldn't do it with Ella, but I want to with you."

"Ella?" Leah stopped, her eyes on his face.

"Ella, my twin. She faced something like you did."

"And?" Her question was soft, almost as if she was afraid to voice it.

"Ella had a stalker, just like you. Only we never knew about it in time. We lost her to him, and I don't want your family to face that." He looked down at her as he tugged her forward to his truck and opened the door, helping her inside. "I don't want to lose you either."

Her eyes followed him as he rounded the front of the truck, her face softening at his words. She had never had anyone express his thoughts like that to her. Then she snorted to herself. Anyone she had been out with ran scared at the first sign of danger.

Leah sat back in her seat at Mac's. "Joseph, you have to stop. I can't laugh anymore."

He grinned at her, no remorse in his look. "Laughter looks good on you."

She shook her head at him. "Stop flirting with me."

He laughed. "Lady, I'm not flirting. I'm dead serious."

She laughed again. "No, you're not." She sobered, looking around. "I can feel something, Joseph, or someone."

He nodded, hating that this had broken up their evening. "I know. If you're finished, we can go." Eyes watchful, he caught Leah's hand as they walked from the cafe to his truck. He could feel that sensation again, the one where he was under observation, and he didn't like it one bit.

Leah turned to him once they were out of the street. "Is there really someone there, Joseph, or I am just imagining it?"

He shook his head. "No, there's someone there, just like yesterday. We need to come up with a plan to keep you safe."

"You sound like Dad. Have you been talking with him?"

"Not strictly about you. Abe and I talked to him about something we've discovered concerning the delivery routes. We're working with him to come up with a way to keep all of you safe." He glanced over at her. "I would like to make you my priority."

She turned, shocked at his words. "Thank you, but you'll have to get by Dad first."

"Already have." Joseph started to laugh as he remember the words Smitty had shot at him that morning.

"What's so funny, or shouldn't I ask?"

"Your Dad. He told me to come see him if I ever became serious about you."

"He didn't, did he?" Leah groaned, mortified at her father's words.

"That won't be a problem, Leah." Leah looked at him shocked. "I may have to go see him tomorrow."

Leah shook her head. "Don't jest about something like this, Joseph."

"Who says I am? I'm just giving you fair warning." His eyes picked up the vehicle coming up behind them, no lights on. "Leah, is your seatbelt fastened and tight?" At her nod, he continued, "We have someone behind us and I need to lose him. Hang on!"

Joseph was boxed in by traffic. When an opening came, he spun the wheel and shot across the opposing lane into an alley and headed down it, turning onto the street at the end and heading in the opposite direction he had been going. Eyes scanning the area and his mirrors, he breathed a sigh of relief. He had shaken his tail, if it had really been a tail, but for how long?

Leah stared at him. "Did you really just do that?"

"Do what? Oh, you mean that driving?"

"Yes! That!"

"Abe makes sure we're well trained. I didn't take a chance. If there had been traffic coming, I wouldn't have done that."

Leah shook her head. "In the process of that fancy driving, did you lose your tail? And I want to learn how to drive like that."

"I did but it doesn't mean he's gone."

She sighed. "That's about what I figured you'd say." She stopped speaking, lost in thought. "Joseph, find us somewhere we can talk. We need to."

Joseph shot her a quick glance, then turned his gaze to the area he was in. Spotting a coffee shop up ahead, he turned into the parking lot. "Do you want to go in?"

She shook her head. "Are there tables somewhere outside where we can sit?"

"There are. Wait here. I'll be right back."

Leah watched as Joseph disappeared into the shop, then came around from the other side. He opened her door and led her to an outside table. Sitting across from her, he waited for her to speak.

She studied the man in front of her, seeking to learn more of his character from his face. She finally nodded. "Okay, so what's the deal?"

"The deal?"

"Yes. The deal. Why? Why you?"

Joseph shook his head. "That I can't answer you, Leah. God alone knows why. Maybe because my sister went through this."

Leah shivered as she looked around. "I still don't feel safe, Joseph. Will I ever?"

"That is my prayer and my aim. So, how do we go about keeping you safe?"

"What did you talk to Dad about?"

He grinned at her. "Besides me coming to see him?" She shook her finger at him. "Okay, Rebel's is working on security upgrades for a number of customers. Micah did a search on something for me, and we've discovered that there are a number of companies we're working with who are on your Dad's delivery schedule. I can't go into specifics, but suffice it to say, it's concerning to us and to your Dad. We're trying to figure out a way to keep all the drivers safe while working on an investigation into who and why."

"I can tell you who. Davies and his cronies. They're working for someone. He always has had a hand in crime and I think he's escalating. Does he think he can use me to get to some of those deliveries or get inside one of those buildings?"

"That's what our guess is. Or use you to get to your Dad and Rory. He may have someone inside one of the companies. We're working on that aspect as well."

"I would suspect he has. Not Tweeter or George from that company." Her eyes grew distant as she thought over the companies and the employees that she knew. She finally shook her head. "There are just too many that I couldn't tell you which one. But for companies, I might be able to. Do you have a pen and paper?"

He shook his head, then handed her his phone. "Use the note taking area and write them down."

"Modern technology can't totally replace a paper and pen. I work better with them." She handed him back his phone and searched her purse. "Okay, so of all the companies we deliver to, these are the ones I would suspect. They have a huge turnover of staff. No one stays there long. It wouldn't be hard to get someone in there and then out. Doesn't the government do background checks before deciding on a company?"

"I have no idea how they work. This is great. I'll pass it on to Jace at Tracker's and also Micah and Abe." He reached for her hands. "Right now, though, I see a lady in front of me who could use some prayers."

She looked at him, astonished, and then nodded. "I could. I just wish Dad would put me back on tows. That would keep me safe."

Joseph was shaking his head at that. "No, it's too easy to fake a broken-down vehicle and get you there on your own."

She blew out a breath. "You're not helping, you know." At his grin, she narrowed her eyes and frowned. "I'm trying to think of a way to keep safe, Joseph. You're not buying that one, are you?"

He grinned at her and shook his head. "Not at all. You're just using this as an excuse to get back on tows."

Chapter 10

Caleb walked through the department, stopping to speak with each officer, then turned to find Frankie and Eddie. Something was up, and he needed to talk to them.

"Frankie, got a minute? I need to talk with you and Eddie."

Frankie looked up as Caleb stopped by his office. "Sure. Eddie's around here somewhere."

"Find him. I'll be in my office."

Frankie watched Caleb walk away, trying to gather his thoughts. He had received some information today that he needed to discuss with Caleb but was unsure how to go about it. He turned to find Eddie at his elbow.

"What's up with Caleb?"

Frankie shrugged. "I have no idea, just that he wants to talk with us both."

Seated in Caleb's office, Eddie watched as Caleb shuffled papers on his desk to find what he wanted.

Checking that the door was closed, Caleb eyed the two men in front on him, friends and colleagues.

"I have just spoken with a government official. Unknown to us, they have decided to share our work on a new contract for armament manufacturing among some businesses in our town. I let them know I wasn't happy we were being informed of this at this stage." He sighed. "I was told it was on a need-to-know basis. However, I have gotten word that someone is aware of this and is targeting the businesses, ready to steal the information and use it against the government."

"And at this stage, the companies are in a mad scramble to upgrade their security and staff?" Eddie's question brought Caleb's eyes to his.

"In a nutshell, Eddie, that's exactly it. Abe's company is working on the security upgrades, and Smitty is working on a plan to provide safety for his drivers as all the companies are ones he delivers to. He's the only contracted delivery service."

"Leah." Frankie's one word drew the men's attention.

"Leah. And Davies." Caleb sat back in his chair, the leather creaking. "Somehow, he must have gotten word as to what's going on and is planning on breaking in and stealing the plans for a key component. Only he doesn't know which manufacturing plant it is. The government has changed its plans as to who is doing what." He sighed. "I just wish they'd talk to us."

"And Davies is planning on using Leah somehow to get in." Eddie stared at Caleb. "That's why he's escalating what he's doing. It's not for something in the past, although knowing him it has to be part of it."

"I'm sure it is." Caleb was frustrated. "I am sure whoever is backing Davies will use her in some way, whether to have her get them in or use her to make Smitty or Rory get them in."

"So how do we keep her safe then?" Frankie's question was one the three were asking themselves. "I know for a fact that she's absolutely terrified of him. I saw her the other night after that incident at Mac's. She's definitely not faking it."

"No, she's never been comfortable around him. My feeling is that any boyfriend she's had has been chased away by Davies. She has never dated anyone for long." Eddie looked down at his hands, then back up. "Where do Abe and his team fit in then?"

"I spoke with Abe earlier. Joseph had noticed how many companies were suddenly upgrading, had Micah do some digging, and came up with the government contracts. Micah's good at that. He's also passed it on to Tracker's for their help. Abe's spoken with Smitty and gotten the schedule for the drivers and the companies. He's passed that on to Tracker's as well."

Eddie sat, digesting what Caleb had said. "And we have no idea who's behind it all. Has Hannah given you a name yet?"

Caleb smiled as he shook his head. "No, and this time I hope the Lord leaves her alone and doesn't tell her." His wife was notorious for coming up with the name of the offender. "Abe is trying to come up with a way to keep Leah safe, but it's almost impossible during the day."

"Unless Smitty locks her in the office, and she won't put up with that." Frankie sat, lost in thought. "Joseph will be around her when he can but that's not during the day, unless he's not working. Can we get Smitty to team him up with her on those days?"

Caleb shrugged. "If you want to ask the two of them and then Leah, go ahead. He already has the security clearances he needs. Abe's men have some of the highest security clearances in the country, as far as I know."

"They do." Eddie spoke up. "His Dad made sure of that and Abe's kept them up. They've needed them for their work."

Leah turned late that afternoon as she heard her name called and footsteps behind her. Frankie was approaching. Just great, she thought, now what?

"Do you have a moment, Leah?"

She nodded. "I guess. What do you need?"

"Is there somewhere we can talk?"

"I'm heading in with my log books. Come on. We can talk in one of the offices."

Seated across from Frankie at a table, Leah studied him. "So, what did you need, Frankie?"

"I'm sure you're aware that security upgrades are going on with some of the companies you deal with." At her nod, he continued. "Caleb has found out that these are related to issuance of government contracts." She watched as he hesitated, pulling together his thoughts.

"Have you talked to Dad or Abe?"

Frankie shook his head. "No. Caleb got the word today, and to say he's not pleased is an understatement." He studied Leah. "To be frank, Leah, you're at risk. Davies has become involved in this. Caleb has word that he's working for whoever it is behind the attempt to get information. And there have been attempts no one saw fit to tell us about." He paused, partly to gather his thoughts, partly by the look on her face. "You don't have to say anything, Leah. Deirdre's been talking. We never knew he was like that with you girls."

Leah shook her head. "No, he hid it well and denied it when asked. He had a dirty little game going on back then, Frankie. That's why some of our high school friends left before they graduated or moved on as soon as they did. They couldn't stomach being in the same town as him." Her gaze centered on the wall behind him, she confessed, "If it hadn't been for Mom and Dad being so much in business here and needing me, I would have left, too."

"I'm glad you didn't, Leah. Now, to keeping you safe. How do we do that?"

She shrugged. "I have no idea. It's not going to be easy. What I'm getting from you is that he'll use me to get in or use me again Rory or Dad. Am I correct?" At his nod, she continued. "It won't make any difference which job I'm doing, will it?" She blew out a breath, frustration evident. "I'm not quitting my job and I'm not working in the office."

Frankie nodded. "We didn't think you would. Abe has come up with an idea and I'm not sure how you'll take it." She kept her eyes on him, watchful but silent. "His men have really high security clearance. What he's suggesting is that one of them ride with you each day."

She shrugged. "It could work, if they want to waste their time that way."

"It's not going to be wasted time, Leah. While they're riding with you, they'll be testing the security that Joseph has come up with and how effective it is. Besides, Joseph will be one of those riding with you." He laughed as her eyes shot to his. "We've picked up on his interest in you, Leah. He's adamant he wants to be part of your security, if not during the day, then at night and on weekends."

She shrugged again. "I don't know about that, Frankie. It's taking them away from their own work."

"Not really. The government has finally realized what's up and contracted with Abe for security. You're part of it as is your Dad and Rory and also your Mom. Your Dad's working on getting some government agents into the loading and storage areas. Someone will be riding with Rory all the time. Your Mom and Dad will have security on them as well."

She sat back, eyes growing larger as he spoke. "This is much bigger than just Davies wanting revenge, isn't it? I didn't realize how big it was." She stopped, then spoke again, "How did he get mixed up in it anyway?"

"That's what we're investigating now. Just know that what we're planning is to try and keep you and your family as safe as we can. You're not to go anywhere without someone with you. And that someone has to be security."

"For how long?" Her voice was barely above a whisper."

Frank shrugged. "We're not sure. The government isn't saying how long it will take to fulfill their contracts but from what Abe was told, it's not a month." Frankie watched her face and the changing emotions chasing one another across it. "Can you work with us for that long, Leah?"

She looked up, fear in her eyes, but determination on her face. "If it means keeping my family safe, then I can." She blew out a breath. "So, who's the first candidate to ride with me?"

Frankie started to laugh. "I think you'll like him."

She stared at him, then began shaking her head. "Don't say Joseph, please."

He nodded, then rose. "Be gentle with him, Leah. He doesn't know what all you do in a day and how heavy a load you carry each day."

Chapter 11

Leah watched as Joseph walked across the parking lot towards her the next morning, dressed in jeans, T-shirt and work boots, baseball cap on head. Why did it have to be him, Lord? Are you trying to tell me something?

"Good morning, Leah." Joseph's greeting floated across the narrowing space to her.

"Good morning, Joseph. Ready to learn to be a delivery driver?"

"That I am. I know I already like who's teaching me." He grinned as she shook her head.

"Flirting again, are you? Don't let the boss catch you."

He held the door, so she could enter and then followed her into the office area.

"Just for insurance purposes, we need this paperwork filled out at some point today.

I just need to verify with Dad what route I'm to take and then we can get busy with the guys loading the van."

Joseph turned as he heard the footsteps behind him and handed Smitty the paperwork. Leah looked at him and then the paperwork.

"You can't be done already," she remarked.

Joseph nodded. "There's a lot of questions on there I can't answer because of my security clearance. Your insurance company is just going to have to live with that."

"I'll talk to them. Given that we're handling government contracts, they'll have to accept that this time." He looked between the two, then said, "Okay, Leah, you have your route. Now, get your coworker busy."

Towards the end of the day, Joseph looked over at Leah as she updated her log. "You really walk a lot in a day, don't you?"

She laughed. "That I do. I certainly don't need to join a gym. How are your feet?"

"They're fine. I'm used to this kind of stuff. This is mild to what I normally do."

She looked over at him. "I guess it is. Who's working with me tomorrow?"

"You're stuck with me for the rest of the week." He grinned at her. "Think you can handle that?"

She rolled her eyes. "I suppose if I have to, I will. Now, this is our last stop coming up. It's always a dicey one for some reason. The shipper/receiver always gives us a hard time, and we can't figure out why."

Joseph's senses alerted, and he looked up at the factory they were approaching, then nodded. This was one that was on Abe's radar. "Do you want me to do the run inside?"

Leah shook her head. "No, I can, but just stay handy, okay?"

"No problem. What do they do about identification of drivers?"

Leah pulled to a stop and then turned to him. "You know, this is one place that doesn't require driver ID and never has. That has always bothered us. We know they have government contracts, but their security is so lax." She thought a minute. "They've never asked you to update theirs, have they?"

Joseph didn't respond. He couldn't answer that question, but if he could, the answer would be a "no". He would have to remember to talk to Abe and Caleb about this plant.

"I see what you mean, Leah," was Joseph's comment when they finished and were back in the van. "Is he like that with Rory or your Dad or any of the other drivers?"

Leah sat back and thought about it. "I really don't know. They've never said. But I've always felt uncomfortable coming here."

Joseph nodded. "Can your Dad switch this one to another route?"

"He might be able to. I'll talk to him." She looked over and grinned at him. "So, newbie, how was the first day?"

He laughed at her. "It was an eye-opener for sure. You really prefer your tow truck to this?"

She nodded. "Strangely enough, I do. There's something about that job that draws me. I know I can't do it forever, but while I can, I want to."

Joseph studied her face and caught the sadness there. "What will you do when you can't?"

She shrugged. "I don't know. Likely work in the office and I hate the thought of that. I don't like being indoors."

"We'll see what we can do about that, then." He laughed as she looked at him, surprise in her face.

"We will, will we?" She shook her head as she parked and gathered up her log book and other gear. "We're done here for now. I'll show you the end-of-day routine. It's not long, just tedious."

Joseph watched as she popped into her father's office and then was back beside him.

"What do you normally do when you're finished?" was his question.

"Whatever I feel like doing, although the past couple of days some gentleman has demanded my time."

Joseph started laughing. "And if this gentleman were to ask for your time tonight, what would the answer be?"

She turned to look at him. "It might be a yes to dinner."

He reached for her hand as they walked through the parking lot. "Where do you want to eat tonight?"

"How about we do barbecue at my place? I have meat I need to use up and fixings for a salad."

"That sounds good. Meet you there?"

She nodded and climbed into her car, watching as he crossed to his truck. *Lord, I have no idea where this is heading with Joseph. And I have no idea where this is going with work. Only You do.*

Joseph stood and watched as Leah worked at her kitchen counter, then approached her, reaching around to snag a piece of cucumber. He didn't immediately move back from her space, instead reaching for a slice of red pepper.

She smiled. "The chicken's over there on the counter." When he didn't move, she tilted her head to watch him. "The lighter is in that drawer over there."

She finally gave him a shove. "Get busy, buster, or we won't be eating."

Laughing, he gave a "Yes, Ma'am" and headed out the door. He scanned her backyard. He didn't like that it was open fields behind her or that her neighbours weren't close. *She really doesn't have a good security area here, now does she,* he thought. Turning to her barbecue, he checked the connections and tubing out of habit, then raised the lid, his hand stilling as he did so. How did this guy find her?

He shot a quick glance behind him towards the door, then sighing, pulled out his phone, snapping a quick picture of the note lying there and sending it on to Abe.

He turned, hesitating, then dialed Frankie's number, knowing he would be disturbing his evening.

Leah, headed out with the chicken, stopped as she saw the look on Joseph's face.

"Joseph?"

He turned and came towards her, leading her back inside the house.

"Joseph, what's going on?"

He sighed. "Whoever is after me left a note for you. Frankie's on his way with a crime scene team."

"What? How did he find me? And just what did that note say?" Leah spun from the counter she had set the meat on and confronted Joseph. "So, you have someone after you too?"

Joseph shrugged. "Four of the team have already been targeted. For some reason, whoever it is goes after a team member and threatens them, but he's really after Abe."

"After Abe? But going after your team? Now, does that make a lot of sense?"

"I guess, in some perverted way, he thinks so. We've never had enough information when we investigate to determine who it is. Even Jace at Tracker's hasn't gotten very far."

Leah shivered and wrapped her arms around herself. "That's scary, Joseph. If the trend continues, he's got what, two more of you before he gets to Abe?"

"That's what we're afraid of. We're also afraid that he will escalate and one of us will be seriously hurt, or one of our friends will be." He stared down at her. "That's why we need to take precautions with you, not just because of Davies. We've been seen together. Abe got a text the other day from when we were in Greentown."

"That's when you felt something, wasn't it?"

He nodded. "It was."

Before he could continue, the doorbell sounded, and Leah headed for it, heart in mouth. Peeking out, she saw a crime scene team standing behind Frankie.

Chapter 12

Frankie watched as the crime scene team scoured the yard and deck, shaking their heads at him. He turned and studied the back of the house and then the sides to the street. When was this note placed, he wondered?

Leah and Joseph stood beside him, apprehension on Leah's face. "Why me, Frankie? Who would be after me, aside from Davies?"

He shook his head at her and pointed at Joseph. "He's why. Matt, Nathaniel, Murphy, Ian. All of them had the same thing happen when they started dating their ladies. So, it's par for the course that you would be next."

"But, we're not dating." She spun to face Joseph. "At least, I didn't think we were."

"It doesn't seem to matter, Leah. Once he sees you with one of Abe's men, that's a confirmation in his mind that you're a couple, and he goes after the couple." Frankie took the bag he was handed. "This is directed at Abe, but it concerns you two." He handed it to Leah.

She took it hesitantly, not sure if she really wanted to know what it said. "Do I really need to know what's here?"

Joseph reached for the bag. "No, you don't, not unless you want to."

She hesitated, then shook her head. "No, I don't want to know. Call me an ostrich if you want, but I have enough to deal with."

Joseph handed the bag back to Frankie, and wrapping an arm around her, led her back inside and pushed her down into a chair in the kitchen. "We need to take precautions now, Leah, more than what we had been doing."

She shook her head. "Absolutely not, Joseph. Just go, will you?"

He watched the emotions chasing across her face. "No, Leah, it doesn't work that way."

The force in his voice brought her head up quickly. Shocked, she opened her mouth to speak, but he laid fingers on it.

"You see, we've been seen together, so it doesn't matter if we aren't ever seen together again. That's how this guy thinks."

Leah sighed. "So what did that note say?"

Joseph studied her. "Do you really want to know?"

She looked up at him again and nodded. "If I'm in danger, I might as well know the whole story."

He nodded, then pulled out his phone to find the picture he had taken. He handed her the phone but didn't release it until she looked up at him. "It doesn't matter what it says, Leah. I still want to date you. But I don't want to put you at risk."

She sighed. "Is this how he wants it, to break us up?" She pulled the phone from his grasp and read.

"Too bad, Finlay, that you don't learn. Another one of your team and his lady. Tsk, tsk, tsk."

She studied it, frown in place, then looked up at him. "It really doesn't say much, Joseph. How do you get that we're in danger?"

He pulled out a chair and sat facing her, weighing his words, not wanting to interfere in the investigation. He heard Frankie come in behind him and wait. "It's like this, Leah. We're not the first ones threatened. He didn't give notes at first, but now he is, whoever he is."

"This is really scary, Joseph. How do you protect yourself from the unknown?"

Frankie spoke from behind Joseph, drawing Leah's eyes to him. "That's the whole problem, Leah. We don't know how to protect these guys and their ladies, although once the couples become engaged, it seems to die down, or else he's playing a waiting game."

"So, if Joseph and I were to get engaged, he'd leave us alone?"

Frankie shook his head. "We have no guarantee that's what would happen. He seems to delight in the unknown, in the terror he can bring on, the fear he feeds to the ladies. He also likes the distress he brings to the team and through them to Abe." He looked over at Joseph as he moved further into the kitchen. "I don't know what to tell you two, except to be very careful. This man doesn't leave a lot of clues, making it very difficult to trace him."

Joseph nodded. "Not even Tracker's has been able to come up with much, and that's unusual for them."

Leah had been lost in thought. "So what you're saying then, Frankie, is that there is someone out there after Abe and is making his team pay?"

"That's a simplified version, but basically that's what we're seeing."

She shook her head. "I don't understand. Why Abe? Who'd he hurt?"

"No one that we know of."

Leah shivered at the thought. "Can we skip through us, bypass who is it with Luke and Micah, and go straight to Abe?"

Joseph gave a half laugh at her comment, then sobered. "If it were that easy, Leah, we'd do just that. Unfortunately, as Frankie says, we don't know who it is. Abe's been upfront with Eddie, Caleb, and Frankie here about his past. You know him too. He doesn't make enemies. Even those people we've dealt with on our assignments aren't enemies, whether or not they like us or not. That's the problem, who is it?"

Leah sat, lost in thought. The two men exchanged glances, then headed for the front door. Joseph stopped in the kitchen doorway, watching Leah.

"Leah, what about your chicken?" She didn't seem to hear him until he asked the second time.

"Oh, the chicken. We haven't had dinner yet."

"No, we haven't. Will the meat keep?"

She nodded. "I'll put it back in the fridge as well as the salad." She looked up, distressed. "You never got your supper, Joseph."

"It doesn't matter, Leah. My main concern is keeping you safe. Now that he knows where you live, it's going to be more difficult."

She looked around her kitchen as she turned from the fridge. "Joseph, where do I go then? I'm not leaving my home."

"What about going to your parents?"

She shook her head. "Not an option, Joseph. Dad's already too protective as it is, and if or when he hears about tonight, it's going to get even worse."

Joseph hated the distress he could see in her face, just because he showed an interest in her. Later that night, hearing her lock up after him, he walked slowly towards his truck. He could feel the evil once again, but which one is it, Lord, he questioned. Which one of us is it directed towards? I want to keep Leah safe and secure, but how can I do that? Is it only her spiritual side that will have security, the security that only comes from You? He stood by his truck, eyes moving and made a decision. Tonight, he would stay out here, watching for anything. Tomorrow would take care of itself. He settled down behind the steering wheel of his truck and pulled out the blanket from the back seat. It would be an uncomfortable night but not the first one he'd spent like that.

Chapter 13

Leah stood on her front sidewalk, coffee cup in hand, staring at the truck parked in front of her home. He really didn't, did he? He really didn't spend the night sleeping in his truck to keep watch? She marched across the lawn and banged on the window.

Joseph lowered the window and grinned at her. "Good morning, Leah."

"Joseph, what did you do?"

He tilted his head as he watched her. "What do you mean, what did I do?"

"Did you really spend the night out here in your truck?"

He looked through the front window, then back at her before nodding. "I did. It's okay. It's not the first time I've done this."

She thrust the cup of coffee through the window at him. "Don't do it again. I don't like it." As she turned to leave, she heard her name called softly. Turning back, she studied his face.

"Leah, I'll do whatever it takes to keep you safe. Trust me on that one. Now, what time do you normally leave for work?"

She looked at her watch and sighed. "About now."

"Okay. I'll follow you."

She stared at him again before turning and heading back for the house. Why, Lord, why he'd do that? Am I really in that much danger?

Joseph parked beside Leah and then waited to walk in with her. She headed for her father's office with him just behind her. He pulled her to a stop before she got too far.

"What are you telling your Dad?"

She stopped, then blew out a breath and shrugged. "What do I tell him? That you found a letter addressed to Abe on my grill? How do you think he'll take that?" Her back to the office door, she didn't see her father standing there, eyes first on her, then on Joseph.

A question on his face, Smitty nodded when Joseph gave the barest shake of his head. They would catch up later and have that discussion Leah seemed to think they should avoid

"All set, Leah?"

Her father's voice behind her caused her to jump and spin around to face him. "Don't do that, Dad."

He gave a short laugh. "I can still scare you with the best of them, eh? I have a treat for you today."

"And that would be?" She was hesitant in her words, not sure what her father was up to.

"You're back on tows today. I need you more there than on deliveries."

Leah's face lit up. "Which truck?"

"The flatbed. And Joseph goes with you. Make sure he has the gear he needs."

She nodded and pushed Joseph back the way they had just walked. "Out to the garage, Joseph, and I'll find gear for you."

"You're happy, aren't you?" He grinned down at her.

She smiled, happy to be back on tows. "I am. I just wonder what made Dad change his mind about me being out there."

Joseph stood back and watched as Leah readied her truck, her whole concentration on the task. He felt Smitty stop beside him.

"Care to explain what that was about earlier, Joseph?" Smitty kept his eyes on his daughter.

Joseph sighed, then nodded. "I guess I need to. Somehow, whoever it is that is stalking Abe has discovered that Leah and I have been out. I found a note directed at Abe on her grill last night."

Smitty was silent, taking in what the implications were. "Is she safe with you?"

Joseph shrugged. "As safe as she can be. This has happened with the other team members who are now engaged. You can trust that I will do everything in my power to keep Leah safe."

Smitty nodded. "I know you will. It's the other people I'm concerned about." He turned to leave, then stopped as Joseph spoke.

"If whoever it is decides to go after me or Leah, it wouldn't make any difference if we stop seeing each other. In fact, it might make it worse for Leah if she denies we're a couple."

"And are you a couple?" A grin peeked through the worry on Smitty's face.

Joseph turned to face him, sincerity in his voice. "I would like to think we are becoming a couple. Your daughter's a hard one to get to stay still long enough to talk to."

Smitty laughed. "She always has been. Just for the record, she's changing back to the happy person she was years ago. And that's your doing, Joseph. Thank you." He paused. "Come see me tonight at home, Joseph. We need to talk."

Leah came up behind Joseph, watching her father walk away, then turning to study Joseph. What had they been discussing, she wondered? I hope it wasn't pulling me off the road totally.

"Joseph." Leah's voice was very quiet and hesitant as she spoke. "Are you ready?"

He turned, a gentle smile on his face. "I am. Where are we heading? I have no idea what you do on a day when you are out in your tow truck."

"It all depends. It can be busy or slow. I usually head out to the centre of town and find a lot to park in for starters. I'll get a call when there's someone needing my help."

"So, it's a kind of hurry up and wait type of work, is it?"

Joseph watched at Leah moved through her day. She was in her element, he decided, providing assistance and help to those who needed it. He was on alert the whole time, watching, scanning the area. He could feel the evil around them, but like before, he couldn't tell where the person was, or even if it was male or female.

He walked back towards the truck, coffees in hand, near the end of the shift, watching as Leah checked her truck once more, then slipped into the cab.

"Where is it, Dad?" He could her voice as she rapidly wrote down an address. "We're off, Joseph. Dad says there's a bad accident, and one of the other tow companies needs my help."

Joseph watched at Leah pulled to a stop behind another tow truck and then got out to approach the driver. The small car was off the road, buried into trees. He studied it, then looked back at the road. Something was off. He walked towards Leah and laying a hand on her arm, stopped her from moving.

"Leah, something's not right here."

She turned to him, surprised at the sternness of his voice. "What do you mean, Joseph?"

"There is no way that car got into those trees from the angle of the tire marks. Not by accident or chance."

The other tow driver nodded. "That's what I was telling Leah. I don't like this. I shouldn't have called her in, but with the angle the car's sitting at, I need someone with a small frame to get underneath to hook it up. None of my guys are that small."

Joseph nodded, taking at look at the name badge sewn on the man's coverall. "Don, I'm Joseph. I've been riding with Leah today. Do you know if anyone is inside?"

Don shook his head. "I couldn't see inside properly, so I'm not sure. I would say not, though."

"Leah, you stay right here. Don't you move." Joseph stared her down until she finally nodded. "This time, you stand back until you're given the all clear. Do me a favour. Put in a call to the police and get someone out here. I'm surprised no one had called yet."

Don shook his finger at Joseph. "That's what I can't figure out. There should have been a police cruiser here when I got here and there wasn't. The call came through the police dispatch."

Joseph stilled in his movements, his mind racing. "With the car in that way, who would know you would need to call in someone to help you?"

Don shrugged. "Just about anyone I guess, but there's no way they would have known I would call Smitty and ask for Leah." Don's voice dropped away. "Unless they set it up so whoever got the call would have to. Leah's the smallest of all the tow drivers and it's known we all call her in when we have something like this." He turned to Leah, eyes narrowing as he studied her. "Who's after you, Leah?"

"Other than Davies, I can't think of anyone." She took a step to the side, studying the car again, then sighed. "Guess what, guys. Guess whose car that is."

"Davies." Joseph turned her and pushed her towards the truck. "Get inside there now and don't come out until I tell you to. You'll have some protection inside there."

"Really, Joseph? Hide in a truck when someone could be hurt down there?"

He stared at her, then hand on her arm, pulled her to the truck, opened the door, and shoved her inside. "I mean what I say, Leah.

Stay there. Be prepared to duck down on the floor if I tell you to. You got that?"

Leah jumped at the bark in Joseph's voice. Scared, she nodded, eyes wide in apprehension.

Joseph turned to scan the area, eyes probing. It was way too open for his liking, and there were numerous spots someone could be hiding. "I mean it, Leah. Don't move from here. This smell of a setup aimed at you. Why, I haven't a clue yet, but that's something I'll be digging into once we're done here."

The sound of gravel crunching, and a vehicle motor had them all turning. Joseph slammed the door shut and walked towards the cruiser. Jake Wilson, who he knew slightly, exited the cruiser and stood staring down at the car.

"How'd they get in that deep?" His voice was incredulous as he studied the car and then the road. "They weren't going fast enough by the looks of it and the angle's wrong."

Don nodded. "That's what Joseph and I were just discussing. He's tucked Leah away in her truck for now. I don't like this, Jake. Something's off here."

Jake nodded. "Have you been down to the car?"

"I went down and took a brief look. I can't tell if someone is inside or not, but given what we've talked about, I would say not."

Joseph stepped away from the two men as he pulled out his phone. It was time to call Abe and ask for help. He quickly ran through what had been going on and what they were now facing.

After hearing what Joseph had noted, Abe turned to Murphy and Luke. "Joseph needs your help, guys. Here's where he is. Bring Leah back here, Murphy. Luke, you stay with Joseph. Either one of them could be the target."

Joseph stood and watched as first the bomb squad cleared the vehicle and then the crime scene team moved in, Frankie standing beside him.

"What's really going on, Joseph? You don't cry wolf over nothing."

Joseph shook his head. "It's not nothing, Frankie, but some of it is classified. It's related more I think to the deliveries Smitty does than someone actually after Leah. She's incidental to what they want."

Frankie glanced towards the truck where Leah was watching the activity, then back down at the car. "Really? What kind of deliveries would they be making?" He held up his hand. "No, don't tell me. If it's classified, it has to be government, and that always causes more of a headache than anything else. Caleb was right."

Leah noted the new vehicle that had approached and stopped near Wilson's cruiser. When one of them headed her way, she reached to lock the door.

Murphy gave a smile as he saw her motion, then stood, his body angled in a such a way he could watch Leah, Joseph, and the area surrounding him. Luke stopped by Joseph, handing him his weapon and holster. It was official, now. Leah was under guard by their team. Abe had tried to avoid it, but it was clear that whoever was after Smitty's deliveries was not above using Leah to get to them.

Joseph headed towards Murphy, determination in his stride, stern lines on his face, Luke keeping pace with him. Murphy moved towards him and the three men stopped, deep in conversation, eyes constantly scanning the area around them. Leah wondered what their conversation was about, then sighed. She knew it was likely about her. She hadn't seen Joseph in work mode before, and it bothered her that the carefree man she had been paired with for the last few days was gone.

Joseph walked to the side of the truck and smiled as she unlocked the door.

"Not too sure on Murphy?" was his question.

She shook her head. "You warned me well, Joseph. I don't know him. Is he on your team?"

Joseph nodded as he looked around, then back at her. "I'm going to be here for a while. I need you to go with Murphy. He's the one you're not sure of. He's going to take you out to Rebel's. Abe's working on something to keep you safe."

"No, I refuse to go." Leah's voice, though adamant in tone, was shaky.

"Leah, you're now under our protection. Abe's been putting it off as long as he can, but the government has been very clear. They know you're going to be used to try and get to those deliveries of your Dad's. Abe's under contract with them over this and he's been told to put you into protective custody, as of now."

Leah stared at him. "Really? I don't think so."

"Leah, you have no choice. You either go with us, or the government security steps in and you're taken away to a safe house. Who knows how long you'd be there. Work with us and that won't happen." Joseph watched her face closely, seeing the fight going on within her.

"What about my parents and Rory?" Her question was barely audible, her fear evident in her eyes.

"We have people with them all the time. Murphy's here to take you to Abe. Go with him, please."

"What about you?"

He smiled again. "Luke's with me. I'll be okay."

She finally nodded and stepped down from the truck. Joseph grasped her hand close in his as they walked towards Murphy.

"Leah, this is Murphy. You'll be safe with him."

She nodded once again and moved away to Murphy's vehicle, looking small and frightened. Joseph's heart broke as he watched, knowing they had no idea of how long this would go on.

Luke watched first Leah, and then Joseph, finally nodding to himself. Well, Lord, he thought, once again a friend has found his lady in the midst of trouble. Help us to keep them both safe and secure. He had no idea of how to do it.

Chapter 14

Watching the activity across from him, he stood under the trees, back far enough that he couldn't be seen. He was frustrated. This should have worked. What went wrong that Joseph's lady didn't go down to vehicle? He looked down at the switch in his hand, knowing that it was useless. They would have found the explosives by now.

Joseph turned as he felt eyes watching him, scanning the area around him. He couldn't see anyone, but he knew someone was there. Who was it?

Frankie stood on one side of him, Luke on the other. Frankie was frustrated. He had just spent the last 20 minutes on the phone with Caleb, who was getting pressure from the government to keep the supplies flowing safely to the manufacturers, without being told exactly what it was he was to keep safe. He knew that Leah was now under protection with Abe's team, under government orders it seemed, but it still rankled that this had been taken out of the department's hands, as much as he appreciated how well-respected Abe's team was.

"Who's with Leah's folks?" Joseph's question was quiet.

"I'm not sure who Caleb has sent but they're safe. As is Rory." Frankie stopped speaking frustration evident. "I just wish we could put all four together and keep them safe that way."

"That wouldn't work, Frankie." Luke spoke up. "Smitty and Rory need to keep the business going, and the government will only deal with Smitty."

Joseph nodded. "They really need to do something about that one plant's lack of security. It has no guard at the entrance. People just walk in and out without any identification on them. I don't see any security personnel at all. My gut tells me that's the most important part of the process too."

Frankie stole a look at him, then nodded. "I'll talk to Caleb and see what he can do. Not much, not likely."

Don walked towards them, an object in his hand. "Frankie, you'll need this. I found it after we pulled the car out."

Frankie reached for the piece of metal that Don handed him. "What is it?"

"That's what I'm not sure of. It doesn't belong on a vehicle, but it was under it. May your lab guys can figure it out."

Joseph and Luke leaned over to see what Frankie was holding, then exchanged a glance.

"I can tell you what it is, Frankie." Joseph's voice had resignation in it. "It's used to set up signals for bomb detonation. When your lab guys take it apart, they'll find a tiny transmitter in it."

Frankie stared at them. "Are you serious?" His face paled. "There really was a bomb set to go off in that vehicle?"

Luke nodded. "We've seen this before. My guess is that Leah was drawn here, and that Joseph would have been down there with her. It wouldn't have killed them not likely but done some serious injury."

Frankie stared at the transmitter, still shaking his head. "What did I just walk into?"

Joseph gave a short laugh. "I don't think any of us know for sure. The government never tells anyone what they're up to. And this time they're placing a lot of lives at risk."

Frankie dropped the transmitter into a plastic evidence bag and then headed for his car. He really needed to talk to Caleb and Eddie on this one.

Joseph headed for Leah's truck. It was time to call it a night, but he knew his night was just beginning. He was exhausted and wasn't even sure how well his brain was working at this point. Luke settled into the seat beside him, watching around outside, then studying him.

"Are you okay, Joseph?"

Joseph heard the concern in Luke's voice. "I don't really know, Luke. Right now, I'm working on too little sleep to even know."

Luke nodded, his eyes scanning the area around them as Joseph headed back to Smitty's. After talking with the night guard and dropping of the tow truck, Joseph headed for his own vehicle, stopping halfway there when Luke placed a hand on his arm.

"Let me have your keys, Joseph. I'll drive."

Joseph's movements slowed by his deep fatigue, he finally nodded and dug out his keys, dropping them in Luke's outstretched hand. "One thing, Luke, let's check the vehicle over before we go anywhere. It's been sitting here all day."

Luke watched as Joseph slumped in the passenger's seat, head back and eyes closed. What has he been through in the last couple of days, Lord? I don't know if I've ever seen him this exhausted. We need him alert and functioning over the next few weeks, and I'm so afraid he won't be. Refresh him, Lord. Give him Your strength.

Parking in Joseph's spot in the compound they all called home, Luke turned to Joseph, then gently shook him awake. "We're home, Joseph."

Joseph roused, then blinked, finally nodding. "Thanks, Luke. It's been a bad day all around."

"That it has." Luke peered at Abe's house, noting the lights still on. "Come on. Let's see if your lady's still up. If anything, I know Ian will have left us some food."

Joseph climbed down from his truck, heading for the house. Luke followed him, concern written all over his face. This was not Joseph, not at all.

Abe turned from the kitchen counter when the two men entered and handed them each a plate of food and a cup of coffee, Joseph hesitating before he finally dropped down into a chair. Abe and Luke exchanged glances, Luke shaking his head.

"How's Leah?" Joseph quiet question broke the silence.

"I think she's finally settled down. She refused to go to bed until she had spoken with her Mom. She was waiting for you to get back, Joseph. Talk to me. What did you find?"

Joseph shook his head. "It's bizarre, Abe. I can't figure it out. When the car had been pulled out, Don, the tow driver who called in Leah, found a bomb detonation transmitter where the car had been. There was someone watching, I just couldn't pick out from where." He stopped, fork in hand, and thought about the day. "It was a set-up, Abe. And I'm not sure which one of us was the target."

Abe nodded. "That's what Caleb said. He's not happy with the government, nor am I. Their secrecy has been all of us at risk, including Caleb's officers. I just wish I had said no to them."

"Is that even possible, Abe?" Luke's question caught his attention.

"It is, Luke. I can say no any time I want. They certainly didn't give me all the information I needed on this, and I have spoken to the one at the top. He got an earful from me tonight."

To hear Abe admit that, both men with him knew the frustration and underlying anger that was there.

Joseph pushed away his plate, not having had much of an appetite, and stood. "I'm crashing in the living room tonight, Abe."

"Thought you would. I left blankets and a pillow on the couch for you."

The two left in the kitchen exchanged glances, then Luke spoke.

"I've never seen Joseph this rough before, and we've been through a lot."

Abe agreed. "It's Leah. That's a new element in his life."

Luke nodded. "That she is. Where do you want us in the morning?"

"I've called a meeting for early morning, here. Go, get some rest, Luke."

Abe wandered through the first floor of his house, checking windows and doors. He hesitated outside the bedroom door where Leah was and, hearing nothing, moved on to

the living room. He watched for a moment as
Joseph slept in deep exhaustion. Like Luke,
he didn't know if he had ever seen Joseph this
tired. He sighed and then turned off most of
the lights, heading for his office. Tonight, the
couch there would be his bed.

Chapter 15

Leah quietly opened the bedroom door early the next morning and listened. She didn't hear anything and moved towards the kitchen, hoping someone had started a pot of coffee. She really needed something this morning and she really wasn't sure it was just a cup of coffee. Movement beside her startled her and she gave a jump and small squeak as she turned. Gideon, Abe's brother-in-law and her friend's husband, stood watching her.

A grin on his face, he pointed to the kitchen. "Good morning, Leah. I hear you need a cup of coffee first thing. There's a fresh pot on the counter."

"Thank you." She turned to head for the kitchen, then turned back to him. "Why are you here, and where are Joseph and Abe?"

Gideon pointed once more to the kitchen and followed her, a smile on his face as she walked ahead of him. She wasn't happy, he could tell, that he hadn't given her any news.

"Sit, Leah." He poured her coffee, setting it in front of her. "What would you like for breakfast? Ian's cooked up some food, and I have a plate here for you. If it's not what you want, tell me." He set the plate in front of her.

The aroma of the food rose, and she sniffed. "This smells good. It will do." She watched Gideon as he sat down across from her. "So, where are Joseph and Abe?"

"They're in a meeting right now with the rest of the team. I'm your security person until one of them comes back."

"I thought you did private investigations, not security."

He smiled as he spoke. "I do security if Abe needs me to. And he needed me this morning. He'll explain what's happening when he comes back."

Leah glared at him, then turned her attention to her breakfast. As she picked up her fork, she sighed. "I'm sorry, Gideon. It's not your fault. I just don't like this."

"Most people who have had to go into protective custody don't like it. You're not the first one to express themselves with a glare and you won't be the last. A glare I can handle. Some people do get violent."

She stared at him. "They do? I couldn't do what you guys do."

"And we couldn't do what you do. So, we're even." He grinned at her. "Now, eat up. I have no idea what's in the plans for the day, but I think you should have some food in you."

She nodded and did exactly what he said, dug into the food. As she tasted the breakfast casserole Ian had made, she stopped, savouring the morsel in her mouth. "Ian made this? His talents are wasted. He should be a chef."

Gideon laughed as he looked behind her, Ian standing there grinning at her. "I think he would prefer to stay where he is, right, Ian?"

Leah's eyes slid closed. "Tell me he's not standing behind me, please?" When Gideon didn't speak, she opened her eyes. "You didn't say anything."

"You told me not to tell you Ian was standing behind you." An impish smile sat of Gideon's face.

Ian shook his head as he moved past the table and then stood leaning against the counter. "Glad you're enjoying that, Leah. I'm Ian, by the way. I don't think we've met."

Leah shook her head. "We haven't, I don't think." She looked around. "Where's the rest of your team?"

Ian and Gideon exchanged glances, then Ian spoke, a grin on his face. "Abe's still talking with some of them. Don't worry. Joseph will be in soon."

Leah glared at him. "Not you, too." She shoved her chair back, rose and headed for the back door, stopping when Ian moved in front of her. "What? I can't go outside?"

"That's something we need to talk to you about, and Abe's the one who will do it. For now, you need to stay in the house."

She turned, frustrated at the lack of freedom of movement, and headed back down the hall to the bedroom she had used the night before. Plopping down into a chair, she sat, glaring at the bed. Why, Lord, why did it have to be me? Couldn't you have used someone else? She knew her attitude was wrong and reached for her Bible. Maybe, somewhere in there, God would have a plan to get her out of here. Then she stopped. No, she thought, that's the wrong attitude. God has allowed this, and I need to make sure my attitude matches what He wants from me.

Flipping through the pages, she stopped at verses she had underlined in the past:

"Isaiah 54:17 No weapon that is formed against you shall be blessed; and every tongue that shall rise against you in judgment, you shall condemn. This is the inheritance of the servants of Jehovah, and their righteousness is from Me, says Jehovah.

"Psalms 46:1 God is our refuge and strength, a very present help in trouble.

"Deuteronomy 33:27 The eternal God is your refuge, and underneath are the everlasting arms. And He shall throw the enemy out from before you, and shall say, Destroy!"

Thank you, Lord, for the reminder, she prayed. Guide us. Keep us secure in You first.

A tap at her door raised her head. Joseph stood there, uncertainty in his manner. She rose and went to take the hand he held out.

"Are you okay?" His question was soft.

"I am, Joseph. Just spending time remembering the security God promises."

She looked up at him. "And you? It must have been late when you got back."

"It wasn't that late, but Abe said you had already retired when we got in." He drew her down the hall with him. "Come, we need to talk with Abe. And I think Caleb or Eddie was on the way out."

She stopped, pulling him to a stop with her. "When does it end, Joseph? When do we go back to our normal every day routine?"

He shrugged. "No one knows, Leah. No one knows but God."

She shook her head. "I can't live like this, Joseph, but if I don't, I might not live. That's the problem we're facing, isn't it?"

He studied her face, seeing the resignation there. "Unfortunately, it is. Come, Abe wants to meet in his office. I hear Ian wouldn't let you outside earlier."

"No, he wouldn't." She sounded grumpy. Then, "I'm sorry, Joseph. I know what you guys are doing and I need to work with you."

Abe looked up from his paperwork as Joseph and Leah entered. Leah wandered around the office for a few minutes, then came and sat in front of the desk, her eyes on him.

Abe's eyes went from Leah up to Joseph, who stood behind her, and then back to Leah.

"How are you feeling today, Leah, other than caged?"

She gave him a quick look and saw the grin he was trying to hide. "You know how I feel, Abe. Caged says it. So, what is your plan?"

"First, Leah, tell me about what your day is normally like." Abe watched her closely as he spoke.

"It depends on which truck I'm in. With deliveries, they're pretty routine: go in, drop off or pick up and then on to the next place. With tows, it can vary widely." She studied him. "Why are you asking?"

"I need to get a sense of what you do in order to come to some agreement with you on how we keep you safe. I've already spoken with Joseph and he's given me his experience with you."

"That last one yesterday was strange. I don't think I've ever had one like that."

"Is it normal for you to get called in like that?"

She shrugged. "Depends on who's doing the tow. Some will call me. Some won't. The majority do though as I always hook up to their vehicle, not mine, and they get the tow."

"Walk me through what you were feeling yesterday at that tow."

She shrugged. "Frustration, anger, then fear. If Don or Joseph hadn't been there, I'd have hooked up the car and pulled it out."

Abe pointed at her. "That's what I'm getting at. You have no fear for what can happen to you when you're out and about. I don't want to scare you, Leah, but you're not aware of what's going on around you. You're focused on your job." Abe locked over as Caleb and Eddie entered, not surprised to see Ben with them. His attention returning to Leah, he continued, "I have been warned that either I keep you safe or the government steps in. You don't want that."

"Why? What will they do?" Leah's defiance was coming through loud and clear.

"What will they do? For starters, they can try and arrest you for being an accessory. At the very least, they'll claim you're a witness and tuck you away somewhere not even your family will be able to contact you. And then they'll keep you tucked away while it goes to trial and through the appeals. This is years we're talking about, Leah, not just a few days." He watched her face whiten. "If you work with us and Caleb, then we can keep you out of the government hands. Trust me. We don't want you tucked away somewhere for years."

Joseph could see the fear building in Leah and he sat on the arm of her chair, his arm going around her. He felt her lean into him, her eyes not leaving Abe as he spoke. Abe had been there before with a witness. The government had swept in and took the witness away. The last Abe had heard, that witness was still in protective custody, not allowed anywhere near his family.

"So, what do I have to do then, Abe?" Leah's voice was very quiet.

"Work with us, Leah. Don't fight us. Help us to keep you away from them and with us." Abe stopped speaking as Ben move over to perch on the corner of his desk.

Leah looked up in surprise to see her uncle there. "Ben? What are you doing here?"

"I'm here because your mother asked me to be. I'm also here because Abe and Caleb asked me to be. This situation is not of your making, Leah. It is what it is. Abe and Caleb have been working on some ideas. Unfortunately, it means you're not out on the road, and I know you too well to think you'll like that." Ben paused, his eyes seeking Joseph's, then turning to stare ahead of him. "I haven't been told their plans, but if it means you staying in one spot for a while, then listen to me for a minute. Use that time to work on those online courses you're always telling me you want to try."

Leah stared at her uncle. "How long is this to go on for?"

Abe spoke up. "The government says three weeks. I say five."

Leah looked at Abe, horrified. "Five weeks? Three is too long."

Joseph's arm tightened around her shoulders. "Abe's is a guess as is the government's. However, if we were to catch those who are after this material, then it would be over."

"Where do we stand on that, Caleb?" Abe's question brought Leah's head around, her eyes staring at the two police officers she had not seen.

Chapter 16

Caleb shook his head. "Whoever these people are, they are keeping themselves well hidden. We haven't had any word yet on any suspects from town or from out of town, and that is very unusual." He paused as his phone rang, then excusing himself, he stepped outside to take the call.

Eddie spoke up. "Frankie's been working his sources on the streets. He's heard some rumblings but no names." He looked straight at Leah. "Leah, we need you to help us with names from the plants. I think that is one way we can try and determine who it is that's after you."

Caleb stepped back him, his face sober. "Leah, I just want you to know that Davies was found this morning."

Her eyes wide, she shook her head. "No, he's not dead, is he?"

Caleb nodded. "He is. The medical examiner puts the time of death to before you were called out to that vehicle."

Leah shook her head, then her whole body began to shake. She didn't hear Ben or Joseph calling her, didn't feel Joseph sweep her up in his arms and head for the house. Ian, standing on watch outside, took one look and went running for Matt, their team paramedic.

Leah clung to Joseph as he tried to lay her on her bed.

"Leah, let me lay you down." He couldn't see her face that she had buried against his chest but could feel the shaking of her body and the tight grip she had on him. He finally sat in the armchair in her room. Ben tucked a blanket around her, then stood back, watching his niece, concern in his eyes and on his face.

Matt stood in the doorway, assessing her from what he could see. "What happened?"

"We got word that the man who had been after her is dead. She just started shaking and isn't responding verbally at all." Joseph's arms tightened around Leah as he spoke.

Matt turned to say something to Abe, then moved forward to crouch down in front of Joseph. "Will she let you lay her down?"

Joseph shook his head. "I tried. She won't let go of me."

Matt nodded. "She's in some kind of shock. With what you've said about yesterday, and now word that the man is dead, it's no wonder. I've asked Abe to call John Thompson and see if he's free to come out. This is out of what I can treat." Matt reached for her hand and she pulled it back so rapidly she almost hit Joseph in the face.

The men stared at each other, then turned to look at Ben and Caleb standing just inside the room.

"What did this guy do to her?" Matt demanded. "She shouldn't be like this over his death."

Ben shook his head. "I don't think we know the whole story but from what Marg has said, it's not pretty. He never touched her, just threatened her."

"Whatever it was, Matt, it was enough to take out a restraining order against him. He tried to kill her by running her down just a few days ago." Joseph once again rose and headed for the bed. This time, Leah let go of him but clutched for his hand. "Ben, is there a way to get her mother out here?"

Caleb spoke up. "I've already asked for that." He turned as he heard steps behind him and then disappeared from the room.

Two hours later, John Thompson stood at the side of the bed, watching Leah, then raised his eyes to her mother, Emily, who sat on the edge of the bed.

"Emily, I've given her a sedative. Hopefully, when she wakes up, she'll be okay." Compassion shone from the eyes of the Emergency Room doctor Matt had called in. He was a good friend to them all.

"Thank you, John. I've never seen anyone like this before. How long?" Her eyes raised to his before dropping back to her daughter, then to Joseph, still sitting beside the bed, Leah's hand tightly gripping his.

John shrugged. "It's hard to say. A few hours at least, I would guess." He turned to leave. "Matt will monitor her and call me if she needs anything more. Don't worry, Emily. She'll be okay."

Emily nodded. "I know, but it's hard not being able to take this from her." She looked up at Joseph, tears in her eyes. "She never ever said what was going on. Why?"

"She's very protective of her family. She is always asking us to make sure you three are safe and unharmed. I would suspect, knowing how these guys think, that he threatened you at some point."

Emily sighed. "I just wish she had told us. She covered it so well, we didn't know. Smitty will be beside himself when I tell him, not knowing so he could take care of it for her."

"I don't think that would have helped, Emily." Caleb spoke from the doorway. "We've had word from others now that Davies is dead. He did the very same thing to them. He thrived on their fear."

Joseph felt Leah's hand finally relax and tucked it under the blanket before he stood. With a glance back at her, he followed Caleb from the room.

"Where do we stand now, Caleb?" Joseph's voice was quiet, but Caleb could hear the anger brewing underneath.

Caleb pointed to the kitchen. "Abe and Eddie are there. Let's sit and talk about this."

Joseph watched as Abe finished off some paperwork, then tidied it into a neat pile before sealing it into an envelope. Abe's eyes raised and studied the men sitting with him.

"Ok, Caleb, where do we stand with Davies?" Abe's voice was brisk.

Caleb sighed. "Not where I would like to be. We have the names of the men he was seen with in the last couple of weeks, but Frankie is having trouble tracking them down. They're from out of town and their arrest record fits with what we've been seeing."

Eddie spoke up. "Davies hid a lot of his activities. We're just finding out now how deep into crime he was. He is certainly connected to the men after the government material Smitty delivers."

"Speaking of the government, how long can we hold them off, Abe?" Caleb's voice was frustrated.

"As long as I have to. I spoke to the man in charge of the security and delivery surrounding this order. He wasn't very happy to hear of what was going on and the lax security at two of the plants. Leah was right on, Joseph, with that last plant. It is the most important part of the order. Government personnel are now in place there and will be until the order is complete."

"How long?" Joseph voiced the question they were all asking.

Abe snorted. "You know the government. They talk in rounds and riddles. I suspect two to three weeks, if that long."

"So, what do we do then about keeping Smitty's family safe?" Joseph was pushing, and Abe knew it.

"Whatever it takes. The government has finally stepped up and put security personnel with Rory and Smitty all the time. They are outside their homes and in the warehouse and office. Emily will be escorted back to their house when she leaves here. We don't want to keep the two women together if we can help it."

Caleb sighed. "Why didn't they just take proper precautions in the beginning, and why didn't they let us know there was a government contract this big going on in town? It would have helped to be able to head trouble off instead of playing catch up."

The men finally arose, a plan of sorts in place. Joseph headed back down the hall to check on Leah and then for the office to work on security plans for a new client.

Abe watched him walk across the yard to the office, then turned to head for his home office. He stopped in the doorway, looking around. He had changed some of it from what his father had had, but he knew he needed to change more. Sighing, he sank into the leather chair at his desk and then unlocking a drawer, pulled out a folder.

He laid the folder on his desk, hand resting on it before he opened it. Leafing through the material, he hesitated at the photograph, a photograph of himself from 12 years earlier with a beautiful red-haired lady. Emma, where are you? he asked himself. I miss you so much. Why did you just pack up and leave like that? That wasn't you.

Chapter 17

Smitty looked up as he heard footsteps approaching him, praying it wasn't the obnoxious government official again. This would be the last time he ever took on a government assignment. With the danger now evident directed towards his family, he was very close to telling the government to go get another delivery service. He would check his contract to see if he could break it.

Frankie and Abe stopped beside Smitty and just watched as the activity level in the warehouse intensified over the next few minutes. It was mid-morning and the drivers were already out on their routes.

"What's up, Frankie?" Smitty's voice was tight, expecting the worst.

"We need to talk with you and Rory, Smitty. Is he around?"

Smitty looked around. "He should be. He was around a while ago." He reached for the mike to the overhead PA system in the warehouse and called for Rory to come to the office.

"Let's wait for him in there. He shouldn't be too long, I hope." Smitty studied the grim faces of the men beside him and groaned inwardly. *What did I do, Lord, when I accepted that contract?*

Rory appeared at his father's office door and when instructed, came in and shut the door behind him, perching on the edge of a chair.

Abe spoke up. "We've been in contact with the government again and told them in no uncertain terms that the contract would be taken from you and given directly to a government delivery service, with no loss of income to you."

Smitty sat back and stared at Abe. "That's not possible. They won't do that."

Abe shook his head. "It's already done. You won't be doing any more deliveries for this project. I've pulled a few strings and made it very clear that this has put numerous people at risk of injury or death. I used my high security clearance to do this. Frankie says the police department PR teams are preparing a statement to release to the press."

Smitty drew a deep breath. "That's a relief. But how do we know we still won't be in danger?"

"We don't know that. The government is to keep their security personnel with all of you until this contract is fulfilled. They're pushing it now that all this has become public knowledge."

Rory and his father exchanged glances. "But we're still in danger, right?" was Rory's question.

"Unfortunately, you are. We have no way of knowing if the men after the material will hear or even pay attention to the media blitz. We need you to still take precautions." Frankie looked around the office. "Leah will need to stay under Abe's protection until the contract is completed and the material shipped out."

Abe looked at Frankie, then spoke. "You know that Davies is dead, right?" At Smitty's blank look, he said, "You knew nothing about how he had terrorized your daughter?"

Smitty looked shocked, then angry. "She said nothing at all. How long had it been going on for?"

Rory spoke up. "I knew she didn't like him, but I didn't know it was that bad. I've asked her and she would just shrug it off. I would say since high school?"

Smitty's head shot around to his son. "That long and no one said a word?"

Rory shook his head. "She never said, and I was never sure."

Abe spoke up. "It's been at least that long, Smitty, and she's not the only one. Caleb says they're getting reports of more than just Leah this has happened to." He stopped, then continued, "When she found out this morning that Davies was dead, she went into shock. John Thompson has seen her and feels she'll be okay. Caleb has Emily with her for now, but we'll be bringing Emily back into town."

Smitty sank back in his chair, devastation on his face. "I never knew, Abe. I never knew, or I would have dealt with it."

"We know, Smitty. Leah has never said, but others have said Davies threatened their family members. That last tow yesterday? It was Davies' car and it was clearly a set up."

"A set up? How?" Smitty was shocked.

"That's what we're working on." Frankie looked at Rory, then Smitty.

"Someone knows how the tow system works here in town. And they've already used it to target Leah and indirectly Joseph."

"They arranged it so Leah would have to be called in." Smitty's voice held anger and helplessness.

"That's about it, Smitty." Frankie paused before he went on. "I was there. The car had a bomb in it, but it was deactivated before it could go off. Joseph says that Don found a denotation transmitter under the car."

Smitty and Rory stared at the two men in shock. "All this related to Davies or to the contract?"

"We think both. Davies was being used to get to Leah, in order to get to you two." Frankie studied the father and son. "We'll never know for sure from Davies' point of view but it's an educated guess that's what was planned. We're still investigating and running down leads."

Rory spoke in a hesitant voice. "I saw Davies with a couple of men I didn't know last weekend. I wonder if they're involved?"

Frankie turned to him. "I'll need you to come down and look through some books for us, at the very least, and maybe work with a sketch artist. We need to find these men before anyone else is hurt."

Joseph headed down the hall towards Leah's bedroom later that afternoon. He hadn't seen that she had been awake and up. He tapped at the partially open door, and then peeked in. Emily beckoned him in.

"How is she?" Joseph's voice was quiet.

"She's been awake, long enough to take something to drink. That was a couple of hours ago." Emily watched as her daughter moved slightly. "I think she should be awake again soon. Joseph, could you sit with her for a bit while I go see if I can find something for her to eat?"

He nodded. "Go ahead. If I know Ian, he'll have something light and easy ready for her."

Emily stopped and turned to stare back at Joseph. "Really?"

He nodded without turning. "Ian's like that. He likes to cook and concoct things for us. Sometimes we have no idea what it is we're eating but it's always delicious."

Joseph sank into the chair beside the bed and watched Leah's face. He knew without a shadow of a doubt that he loved her, even after such a short period of time. Now, to keep her safe until he could find out if she felt the same. Lord, she's such a precious lady. Keep her safe, please, dear Lord.

Leah stirred, her head feeling groggy. She frowned as she opened her eyes, not sure where she was. Glancing around through half-open eyes, she saw Joseph sitting by her bed, head bowed. She looked at him in confusion, not sure what was happening.

"Joseph?" Her voice was barely audible, but it brought up his head.

Joseph studied Leah's face, seeing something different in it. She no longer had the fear etched in it that she had, he thought.

"Hi. How are you?"

She stretched out her hand. "All right, I guess. I just don't understand why I'm here. The last I remember was talking with Abe." She stared at him again, eyes puzzled. "What happened?"

"What happened? You went into shock, Matt says, when you found out Davies was dead. We called in John Thompson to come see you."

She stared at him in horror. "Davies is dead? For real?" At his nod, she closed her eyes. "For real. No more threats. No more watching wherever I go in case he shows up."

Joseph tilted his head. "Did he do all that?" At her nod, he shook his head. "No, no more of that." He turned his head as he heard a noise in the hall. "Let's get you sitting up a bit. Your Mom's here and I think she's found some food for you."

Chapter 18

Joseph went on a search for Abe. He needed to know what the next step was and how they would proceed.

"Where do we stand now, Abe?" Joseph's question brought Abe around from his computer.

"Come in and sit, Joseph. First, how is Leah?"

"She's awake and alert. Her Mom was getting her some food." Joseph kept his eyes on Abe. "So, where are we now?"

Abe sat back and sighed. "The government's taken over the deliveries, we still have agents with her family and in the warehouse. But I still don't think she's safe."

"I agree. I think she can still be used against Smitty somehow. So, what do we do?"

Abe shook his head. "That's what I'm working on. We still have to keep her in our care until whatever the government is working on leaves town."

"And the timeline on that?"

Abe shrugged. "It keeps changing every time I speak to someone. It's frustrating." He looked towards the door, frown in place. "Caleb is beyond frustrated. He had no idea something this big was going on in town. Frankie's working his sources to find answers to Davies' death but isn't getting too far. He says everyone he talks to is scared, just like Leah was."

"How does someone have that much power over a person?" Joseph stopped. "It's because there's someone in town, high up likely in the government, who is controlling things."

Abe shot him a look, then turned back to his monitor. "I think you're right. That's what I was working on when you came in. I have about three names I need to get information on."

"Let me have them and I'll get them to Tracker's."

Abe nodded. "They're the best for doing this. I don't want to involve Gideon in this if I can help it."

"No, I didn't think you would want to. I'll head in there today."

As Joseph stood to walk away, he stopped with his hand on the door handle as Abe called to him. "Take someone with you, Joseph. You're not safe either."

Joseph spun to study Abe. "What do you mean?"

"It's become apparent to everyone since that incident this morning that you're very important to Leah, whether she realizes is or not. She is to you, too. They'll use that against you two." Abe watched as Joseph mulled this over, then closed his eyes.

"You're right, Abe. Thanks for the reminder."

Late that afternoon, Joseph sat in his truck, fingers idly tapping the wheel, lost in thought. Murphy watched him quietly, finally speaking.

"What's the problem, Joseph?"

Joseph started, then looked over at Murphy, a perplexed expression on his face. "I don't understand it, Murphy. If Davies is dead, then who was he working with? There had to be someone."

Murphy nodded. "I know. Did Jace give any clue yet as to what he had found?"

Joseph shook his head. "Not yet. I'm not sure how much he's been able to dig up." He sat for a minute longer, then turned to Murphy. "If it was you, where would you start?"

Murphy studied his hands, looking for wisdom to answer Joseph. He finally looked up at his friend. "I don't really know, Joseph. There's just such a lack of information available. We knew Davies had friends with him, but who are they? Frankie's not able to find out much on them at all."

Joseph pointed at Murphy. "That's what's bothering me, Murphy. Why can't we find out any information on them?"

Murphy nodded. "I know. It's puzzling. What does Abe say?"

"He's puzzled, frustrated, worried. He knows something's going on, but he can't pinpoint who or what. Caleb's the same." Joseph blew out a breath. "I just wish I knew what I could do to help."

Murphy stared out the window at the gathering dusk. "I wish I knew what we could do for you and Leah, Joseph. They're not letting her go back to driving, are they?"

Joseph shook his head as he put the truck into gear and pulled away from the shoulder of the road. "No, Abe and Caleb are adamant that she not drive. Smitty's in agreement." He sighed. "And that will hurt her. Driving is part of who she is."

Murphy hesitated before he spoke. "I know she'll not be happy. But look at it this way. God is in control, Joseph. He has a plan. Right now, that plan is to keep Leah and her family safe and secure."

Joseph agreed. "I know. But try telling that to her. We've had conversations like this over the couple of days I rode with her. She's not ready to accept that yet. That scares me. My feeling is that she'll get a call and just go without telling anyone."

"You really think she would?"

Joseph nodded. "I know she would. She was ready to go down to that car without a second thought and would have if she hadn't been stopped."

Murphy shook his head. "She has no fear. That's concerning." Murphy turned to study Joseph's profile. "But there's more to it than that, isn't there?"

Joseph hesitated and then nodded. "There is, Murphy. We never talk much among ourselves about our families and what's happened in the past. My sister, Ella, had something similar to Leah, only hers didn't turn out well."

Murphy's eyes slid shut. He knew what was coming. "How long, Joseph?"

"Two years. During that time, my Dad had a heart attack. He's never been able to work since. It just about tore my family apart." Sadness covered his face. "The worst part is I should have known. Twins are supposed to have this connection, and I never knew. I never felt anything."

"And you're afraid of that happening to Leah, aren't you?"

Joseph nodded. "I am. I never want to see another family go through that." He pulled up to the security compound and turned off the truck. "So, how do we keep her safe, Murphy? She doesn't think like we do. She's never had worry about her security like we do for our clients."

"No, she never has. Let's see what Abe and Caleb have come up with." Murphy hesitated before climbing down, then shook his head and headed for Abe's home, Joseph walking step in step with him.

Caleb was late getting out of the office. Frankie tracked him down finally.

"What do you have?" Caleb motioned him into his office.

"We've got word that two of the men seen with Davies are in town. I'm taking three officers and heading for the bar they're in. Hopefully, we can begin to get some answers."

Caleb nodded. "I'll be here for a couple of hours. If not, track me down at home."

Frankie's eyes watered from the smoke in the bar. How can anyone smoke, he wondered? He saw Jake Wilson standing near the bar and two other officers waiting around the edge of the room. Wilson nodded towards a table near Frankie where two men sat, numerous empty glasses in front of them. Frankie approached them.

With little resistance, the two men were asked for identification, then hauled to their feet and out to be placed in the back of the cruisers.

Wilson approached Frankie. "Why did that go so smooth?" His gaze scanned the area. "It doesn't feel right."

Frankie agreed. "I know. They were just waiting for us to come get them. When they sober up, we'll talk to them, but I have a feeling we'll not get much. I'm not even sure who well they knew Davies." He too scanned the area. "I don't like this, Wilson. There's

someone out here watching us. Let's get out
of here before something happens."

Chapter 19

As Abe approached him the next morning, Joseph turned from where he was scanning the hills and rocks surrounding the yard. He felt someone out there, but where and who?

"Joseph, Frankie called. They picked up two of the men who were with Davies, but he thinks there are more out there."

"That's good, I guess, but that still doesn't solve the problem of who's out there." Joseph pointed to the area around them as he turned back to watch. "Someone is out there, Abe. I can feel him."

Abe nodded as he too watched the area surrounding his home, eyes narrowed against the morning sunlight. "I know there is. It concerns me that we don't know who it is."

The watcher lowered his binoculars. He didn't want the sun to reflect off them, but he needed to know what Abe was planning.

He turned to look around him, sensing someone near. Hearing a click behind him, he spun. Nathaniel stood there, weapon drawn and pointed at him.

"Let's rise very slowly. Hands in the air." Nathaniel's voice was grim. He whistled and he heard an answering whistle from his left. Ian was there beside him quickly.

"Frisk him, Ian, and then we'll take him down to Abe."

Searching the man produced no weapons or identification. Puzzled, Ian and Nathaniel exchanged glances, then Ian shoved the man forward.

"Get moving. We're heading down to the yard you're so interested in."

The man cursed softly to himself. How had he been so careless? His employer would not be happy, but there was no link between them. All communications had been done secretly and all payments were in cash. All they had on him was trespassing.

Abe spun as he caught movement out of his eye and stood, stern lines forming on his face, as he watched Nathaniel and Ian approaching, the man they had discovered in front of them. What was going on?

"Look what or who we found, Abe." Nathaniel's voice was tight and angry.

Abe studied the man. He didn't know him, or did he? He looked familiar somehow.

"So, you're trespassing and spying on us. Who are you working for?" Abe's voice was tight with controlled anger.

The man stared ahead, refusing to answer. Abe sighed, then turning to Joseph, said something quiet.

An hour later, Caleb stood in Abe's office, watching as his officers shoved the man into a cruiser and then headed for town.

"He had no identification on him, Abe. He's not from here." Caleb was frustrated.

"I know. Ian looked for a wallet when he searched for weapons and didn't find anything. Some of the guys have gone looking for a vehicle." Abe paused, leaning back in his chair, and stared ahead. "Who was he after: Leah or me?"

"That's what I want to know. Somehow, though, I get the feeling he's not talking. We can hold him for a while but not for long." Caleb turned to face his friend. "You both still need to take precautions. This is far from over." He turned as Eddie entered the building. "Did you get anything from him?"

Eddie shook his head. "No. He's not talking. But I know him from somewhere, though. He looks familiar."

Abe shook his head, a frown on his face. "I didn't recognize him. I would like to know who he's working for and why."

Caleb headed for the door. "Like I said, somehow I don't think we'll figure that out."

Eddie studied his nephew, concern in his eyes. "What are you thinking, Abe?"

Abe drew a deep breath, then turned to his uncle. "I really don't know, Eddie. I have a feeling I've seen him somewhere, but I just can't place him. And it's that fact that's so frustrating."

"We can hope his fingerprints are in the system somewhere, but I wouldn't plan on that." Eddie looked towards the door. "Where's Leah?"

"Joseph and Luke are with her in the house. She's starting to feel caged and I can't say I blame her."

Eddie shook his head, his eyes sad. "No, I can't say I would either." He studied his nephew. "How about Marg and Peg come out for a while today? Would that help?"

"It might. I know she really misses her Mom, even though they manage to talk every day." Abe shot a glance at his uncle, then to the door. "I think the four guys are planning on bringing the ladies out tonight or tomorrow night for a girls' night in as they call it. That will help. Rebecca's involved in it as well, and I think she's bringing in Rachel, Gideon's sister, too."

"That will help." Eddie continued to watch Abe. "How are you really doing, Abe? This with your men, it's hitting you hard."

Abe sat back and scowled at his uncle, then sighed. "It is. It's frustrating seeing what they're going through. It hurts that I can't stop it. And sometimes I wonder where God is in all of this."

"Right where He's always been, Abe. I know this is testing the faith of each one of you and I see you all coming through stronger than ever. Murphy has it right when he says no one knows the plans or purposes of God in all this." Eddie stood and headed for the door, hesitating for a minute. "I don't mean to pry, Abe, but what happened with Emma?"

Abe shot him a look, then shook his head. "I have no idea, Abe. Not a one. One day she was there, the next she was gone."

Eddie nodded, knowing there was a lot more going on than what Abe said. He had never met Emma, but he had seen firsthand the devastation Abe had gone through. His heart raised in prayer for his nephew, he turned and walked away. He knew Abe wouldn't say much more than he had.

Joseph turned from the living room window, eyes thoughtful, a frown on his face as Ian entered. "What's going on, Ian?"

"Frankie's taking him in but doesn't think he'll get much from him. Abe keeps saying he looks familiar, as does Eddie." Ian stared into the distance, trying to puzzle it out. Then he turned to Joseph. "If we show Leah a picture, do you think she'll recognize him?"

Joseph shrugged. "Who knows at this point. Do you have a picture of him?" He reached for Ian's phone and then turned to head for the kitchen, stopping at Ian's quiet words.

"Even if she recognizes him, Joseph, she's still in danger. We don't know who he's working for." Ian watched with compassion as Joseph's eyes slid shut, then opened again, his face hardening into stern lines.

"Now I know what you felt like with Lydia. It's not fun, is it?" Joseph walked away before Ian could respond.

Ian paused for a moment for prayer, then headed after Joseph.

Leah turned from the back door she had been staring out, her face breaking out in a smile when she saw Joseph approaching her. Then her smile faded at the grim lines on his face. Her eyes dropped to the phone he held.

"No, Joseph. No. Don't tell me it's one of my family."

Joseph heard the worry and pain in her voice and mentally kicked himself for approaching her that way. "No, it's not, sweetheart. Ian and Murphy found someone watching the area this morning. Ian has a picture here he wants you to take a look at and see if you recognize him." His eyes watched as her face shifted from concern for her family to puzzlement.

"Why would someone be watching here?"

"That's what we're trying to understand. He had no identification on him." He handed her the phone.

Hesitatingly she reached for it, her eyes studying Joseph's face. Then she looked down and froze.

"I know him. He's been in the office, sending parcels. Give me a minute and I'll come up with dates and times for you."

Ian and Joseph exchanged a quick glance, then Ian headed for the office outside to find Abe. Was this the breakthrough they had been praying and waiting for?

"You know him?" Joseph's voice was incredulous.

"I've seen him, rather than know who he is. I seem to recall that he didn't start coming in until we started with the shipments for the government." Leah's eyes grew thoughtful. "I don't remember that he ever gave a name. Or just what it was he was shipping. I think it was just an envelope." She looked up at Joseph. "Can we send that on to Mom? She works in the office and might remember more than I do."

"We can do that. What's her number?" Leah provided it to Joseph and watched as he sent the picture on.

Chapter 20

Abe tracked Frankie down later that afternoon. Frankie looked surprised to see him, then waved him into his office.

"How come you're here?" Frankie watched as Abe settled back into his chair.

"Leah's Mom came up with a name for our friend from this morning. Leah recognized him as sending packages through their delivery service." He handed over the name. "I'm not sure if it will help you any or not." He started laughing, and Frankie stared at him. "Leah had an interesting comment. She said to check his shoes, people hide stuff in them."

Frankie blinked, then started to laugh too. "I would never have thought of that." He stood and leaving the office, spoke to Wilson. "Wilson will look after that for her. That would be too easy, you know."

A few minutes later, Wilson appeared at Frankie's door, shaking his head. "We need her on our investigative team, Frankie. She was right."

Frankie looked shocked, then asked, "What did you find?"

"Money, a driver's license, and a credit card. We're checking that information now to see if it matches him or not."

Abe was laughing as he stood. "She'll never let us forget this, you know. Let me know what you've found out and if he's really after Leah."

Frankie looked after him, then up at Wilson. "There's something you didn't say when Abe was here."

Wilson nodded. "I also found this." He handed over an evidence bag with a sheet of paper that had been folded very small. "This guy wasn't targeting Leah. He was after Abe."

"What?" Frankie's shocked look was quickly schooled back to neutrality as he turned to read the note. "Is this for real? Who's after Abe?"

Wilson shrugged. "Eddie says Abe has no clue. This really doesn't help us either."

Frankie took a second look at the note which contained a detailed map of the security compound, Abe's name, and a monetary amount. "I don't like this, Wilson. Let me take a picture of this and then get it to the lab."

Frankie stopped beside Caleb as he stood in the break room. "I've got some new information for you from this morning." He handed Caleb his phone opened to the picture of the note.

Caleb studied it, then studied Frankie. "Have you gotten anything from this fellow?"

Frankie shook his head. "No. He's not saying anything. He won't confirm a name. We can hold him for a while longer and then we'll have to charge him as a John Doe."

Caleb nodded. "Has Abe seen this?" At the negative shake of Frankie's head, Caleb paused. "We need to let him know about this. I don't like this, Frankie. I wish I knew who is was." As he turned to walk away, Frankie spoke.

"We found a driver's license and some cash hidden in his shoe." Caleb turned back, eyebrows raised as Frankie began laughing. "Leah suggested we check his shoes. Her mom also provided a name for him that we're looking into. Apparently, he's shipped envelopes through their company."

"That would be too easy." As the two men walked back to Caleb's office, Caleb asked, "Where do we stand with Leah?"

"Not where Eddie or I would like to be. Right now, we're at a standstill. She's getting restless."

"Has Abe considered letting her go back to work at the office instead of on the road? It would be easy to provide security for her there."

Frankie stared at Caleb, thoughts running through his mind. "I don't know if he has. He hasn't said. I know he has a team coming in next week for training, so how he'll manage the two I don't know."

"I'll talk to him and see what his feelings are." Caleb paused, chasing a thought through his mind. "If she comes out of hiding, it may bring out the ones after her and we can end this."

"That's my thought, too, Caleb. But I know Joseph will be opposed to that."

Caleb grinned at Frankie. "Like that, is it? They're well suited to one another. Keep me informed."

Hearing laughter from the kitchen, Joseph headed that way, wondering what was up.

"Get your own, buster. That's mine!" Leah's cry of outrage greeted him as he stood in the doorway.

Micah and Ian were laughing as Leah gathered back the cookie dough Ian had tried to steal from her.

"What's going on in here?" Joseph's voice broke into the noise.

Leah looked up, a huge smile on her face. "We're trying to bake cookies and your team mate keeps stealing mine."

Ian stood, hands in the air, laughing hard enough he couldn't talk. Leah shook a finger at him, then turned to Micah.

"And you're no help. You're supposed to be guarding me and you're aiding and abetting Ian's stealing."

Joseph stood, shaking his head at their nonsense. It was good to see Leah laughing, he thought. It had been a hard few days for her. He reached for some cookie dough and ended up with his fingers smacked.

"That's mine. If you want your own, make it yourself."

Joseph laughed at her, then wrapping an arm around her shoulder, said, "How be you get cleaned up and let Ian and Micah finish off what few cookies are left to bake? Abe wants to talk with you."

Her body stilled, and she looked up at him in apprehension. "Is it good news or bad news?"

Joseph shared a look with Ian and Micah before he answered. "It depends on how you look at it. You might think it's good news. I'm on the fence about it."

Joseph caught Leah's hand in his as they walked over to the office. He knew what Abe wanted to talk to her about and he was adamant that he didn't want to put her out there in danger. Why, Lord? Why can't we just keep her safe and secure without having to put her into danger again?

Abe looked up from his paperwork as Joseph and Leah entered. Here we go again, Lord, he thought. How do I do this? How do I fulfill my commitment to the government, keep Leah safe, and still bring in that team next week for training? I just feel so overwhelmed right now and it's only the beginning of the week.

Leah perched on the edge of a chair, watching the conflicting emotions cross Abe's face. She knew they were strong emotions if he showed them.

"Okay, Abe, what's up? We've been friends for too many years to let you hide what you're thinking." Leah's question broke through the silence in the room.

Abe sighed and sat back. "Wilson wants to hire you as an investigator, you know. You were right on with that bit about the shoes."

"I was?" Leah was surprised. "I was only joking, you know. That's what they do in the movies."

Abe smiled. "Joking or not, they found some identification in his shoes. Now, Frankie has talked to your Mom, but she couldn't give much information on the man. The name and address he gave weren't correct."

She snorted. "Did he really think they would be? Of course, they wouldn't be." She eyed him as he concentrated on his desk. "That's not what you want to talk to me about. Spill it, Abe."

Joseph had to keep a smile in check. She was getting feisty, he thought, being cooped up. His mind went to the scene he had come upon in the kitchen. Poor Ian, he thought. I don't suspect he ever thought she would act like that with him. He listened as the conversation continued, torn between what he wanted and what he knew needed to be done.

Abe shook his finger at her as he smiled. "Behave, Leah, or I won't tell you." He sat back as he watched her, his eyes catching the look on Joseph's face as he stared at Leah. Mentally nodding, Abe thought, Ian was right about Joseph's feelings for Leah, and that would make this so much more difficult for him to decide the best method to go with.

"Leah, you're still under our security protection, thanks to the government. However, I know you're chafing under it. Caleb has a suggestion, and I will tell you right now, I'm not happy with it or even comfortable talking to you about it."

"It must mean I'm being sprung, if you're not happy." Leah's quiet comment brought Abe's eyes up to her.

He sighed. "In a way, that's about what it is." He hesitated, knowing his next words would not make anyone happy. "Caleb has suggested that we let you go work in the office at your Dad's warehouse. Smitty told me that it's getting harder to keep up with both he and Rory on the road." He stopped once again, eyes watchful. "What it would mean is that you're putting yourself out there for someone to come after you. I'm not sure any of us are happy about that choice."

"Would I still have to stay here at nights? How would I get back and forth? Would any of your team be there during the day?" Leah's questions spat at him faster than he could catch them.

He held up a hand. "One question at a time. We need to think this through and plan. If you do go back, you need to understand just how dangerous it can be. Even though your Dad's not doing the deliveries for the government any more, your family is still at risk."

"I get that, Abe, and I think my parents and Rory do too. Right now, we're not able to see one another really. That's not who we are. We all want this over with. If it comes to putting myself out there as a target, then, yes, that's exactly what I will do." Leah's voice was steady. The two men knew she had likely been thinking through what she found herself in and the options available for her.

Joseph's eyes were locked on Leah. Abe watched as the emotions chased each other across his face before he reined them in and set his impassive look in place.

"We have to set some ground rules, Leah, that you will need to adhere to. Putting yourself out there just doesn't risk yourself. It risks everyone around you."

"Again, Abe, I get that. What is the plan?" Leah was not backing away from him.

Abe hesitated once again, then spoke. "What we would like to do is have you go work in the office with your Mom. That way, your Dad and Rory can go back to their deliveries. Your Dad says he's fine for tow drivers right now, but short on delivery drivers. He is adamant he will not let you out on the road until this is settled."

She nodded. "I can agree with that. What else?"

Abe was stunned. He had expected a fight from her. "I want to place two of my men with you at all times when you're there. I know you are familiar with all the employees there and trust them. I don't know them and therefore, I don't trust them. There are also customers coming in and out. We have no idea who it is that's trying to get to you. If we did, we wouldn't be having this conversation."

"I get that as well, Abe. Back to my question, where do I stay when I'm not working? Here or at my own home?"

"Here. It's the best place to keep you secure."

"Really?   After your guys finding someone up there spying on you?"

"Leah, please. That guy was after me for some reason, not you." Abe's face grew grim. "It's you that we're talking about right now."

She held up her hands. "Again, I get that. Just tell me what you're planning."

"We've made arrangements for you to start back at work tomorrow. Joseph and Ian will be with you tomorrow. Joseph will stay with you in the office. Ian will be floating in the warehouse. Your Dad is coming up with a cover for him. If we need to switch one of them out, your Dad has already made plans for that." He watched her face. She wasn't giving anything away. "On Friday, you'll have Joseph and Micah, as Ian has to be here. Next week, we'll work out what we're doing to have some of the team with you."

Chapter 21

Late in the afternoon on the Friday, Micah stopped beside Joseph, watching Leah as she moved around the service counter.

"Does she ever stop?"

Joseph shot him a quick look and then grinned. "Not that you would ever notice. This seems to be her normal speed." He looked around. "She's locking up tonight, she tells me. We'll need to make sure we're with her when she does."

Micah nodded and headed back for the warehouse. He didn't feel comfortable today. He could feel the presence of evil somewhere and wanted to make sure all the employees were accounted for before Leah came out to the back.

Leah looked up as Joseph leaned against the counter beside her. "This is the end of it for the day, Joseph. We can go in just a few minutes."

He nodded as he looked around the reception area. "What all is involved in closing up?"

"It's easier if I walk you through it. I need to lock the cash into the safe in Dad's office, first. If you can lock the front doors that would be great."

Joseph followed her through the office area to Smitty's office, senses on high alert. Like Micah, he could feel something. Once she turned from locking the safe, he approached her, standing in front of her to keep her from moving away, hands going to her upper arms.

"Now what?" His eyes searched her face.

Startled at his proximity, she looked up. "I have to walk through the warehouse and make sure all the doors are locked. It takes about 20 minutes to do that. And while I'm doing that, I check the offices to make sure everything set for the weekend. Lights off, computers down, that kind of thing."

"Okay, let's go. But first, you need to stay with either myself or Micah."

"Joseph, everyone's gone. You saw them all check out when they left."

He nodded. "I know what I saw, but I also know what I feel. Something's off, Leah. This is what Abe was talking about when he warned you."

Leah stared at him for a minute, a frown drawing down her eyebrows, then she sighed. "I still don't have freedom, do I?"

Joseph shook his head, just for a brief moment letting his growing feelings for her show. "Not like you've been used to. Trust me when I say that I want this over as much as you do. There's a lady I would like to get to know a lot better and it's really difficult when I'm on her security team."

She looked up at him, a small smile on her face. "You would, would you? Well, we'll just have to see about that. Now, turn around and walk towards the warehouse. I would like to leave at some point tonight."

"Micah's out here somewhere." Joseph watched carefully as she started her walkthrough. As she approached one of the big doors at the back, Micah headed her way.

"Leah, there's something off about one of these doors. The security system is saying it's not closed, but it's closed tight."

Joseph and Micah exchanged glances. "Who would have known you were closing up tonight?" was Micah's question.

"Any one of the employees and anyone watching the warehouse and not seeing me leave yet." Leah looked between them, apprehension in her glance. "This is what you mean, isn't it?"

Joseph nodded. "I need you to take a look at the door. You know how it's supposed to be. I'll take a look at the security lock, to see if it's been tampered with."

"Tampered with? You mean by an employee?" Leah stopped, shock on her face at the thought. "Wait a minute. Is that why you two are here with me?"

"Not totally. Abe has your Dad pulling employee records and going through them. Somehow, someone has been approached to attempt to get to those deliveries we keep hearing about. And don't think for a minute they won't hesitate to use you to get them." He felt sadness run through him at the look on her face. "I'm sorry, Leah. I know you all consider the employees as part of your family. We're trying to prove that none of them would hurt any of you."

She nodded, then turned with determination and headed for the door, Micah and Joseph on either side of her. She unlocked it and grabbing the chain at the side, pulled it open. "We need to check the track on either side and along the bottom to make sure the sensors are still there and that no debris has gotten stuck. That can happen just by deliveries going in and out."

Finding the tracks clear, Joseph reached for the chain and pulled the door back down and locked it. "Did the sensor go off again, Micah?"

"Looks okay, but I'll let you check out the panel for sure."

Joseph turned to the panel, then stopped, his hand going to the weapon at his waist.

Micah turned as well. "Leah, is there anyone other than us here?"

"There shouldn't be, Micah. Once the doors out here are locked, everyone has to go out through the front and punch their time cards out. I didn't see any that weren't punched out." She stopped, glancing around. "But this with the door, that concerns me. We haven't had any issues with the doors in a long time. All the employees are good about checking for debris and wear. Dad set up a reward program for things like this. If an employee reports an issue, they either get a bonus or time off."

"How easy it is for someone to slip in and hide?" Joseph was moving slowly towards where the noise had come from.

"Not very easy. Everyone in here has to wear a badge and if someone doesn't, then the security system picks it up."

Micah and Joseph's eyes met over Leah's head. This meant that someone had circumvented the security system or else an employee was still on site.

"Leah, we need you to stay right between us. If we tell you to hide or run, do it without question. Got it?" Joseph's voice though low, was harsh and firm.

Leah jumped at the tone in Joseph's voice and stared between Micah and him. She nodded, unable to say anything.

"I sent a text off to Abe, and he's been in touch with Caleb and Frankie. They're on their way." Micah's voice was barely above a whisper.

"Is that really necessary?" Leah's voice was angry. "We don't know if someone is even in here."

"Leah, this is what we do for a living." Joseph's answer was patient despite his growing conviction they were not alone in the building. "We've had this feeling before and it has saved our lives. Let us do our job. Part of that is to keep you safe."

She finally nodded and kept in step with them as they moved quietly through the warehouse. A sudden scuff of sound stopped them in their tracks. Joseph pointed at himself and then to the left. Micah nodded and gripping Leah's arm, pulled her to the right and out of sight into an alcove, standing in front of her, weapon drawn.

Leah caught her breath at the realization of how real the danger was. She had heard what Abe and the others had been saying, but it hadn't really sunk in until now. Lord, she prayed. Keep us safe. Don't let anyone get hurt. Protect us.

Micah searched the dimness of the warehouse, looking for someone, anything that shouldn't be there. He knew Joseph would be searching everywhere he could but there were just too many places someone could hide.

His weapon raised in front of him, Joseph approached the end of a row of pallets, stopping to catch his breath and listen. A whisper of sound came from behind him, and then darkness closed in on him as he fell forward, his weapon spinning across the floor away from him. The dark figures stood over him, motioning. Two lifted him and headed for the door near them while two others headed back the way Joseph had come, feet silent, eyes watchful.

Micah watched and listened. He could hear nothing but his own breathing and that from Leah behind him. Where was Joseph? He glanced down at his watch. It had already been 20 minutes and he should be back. He partially turned to whisper to Leah when he too went down into darkness, Leah's scream the last thing he heard.

Leah fought with her abductor, scratching, hitting, kicking, until he wrapped his arms around her and just picked her up. She still struggled but to no avail. Who was it, she wondered, and where was she being taken?

Set on her feet outside near a van, her hands were roughly pulled in front of her and bound with coarse cord. A blindfold and gag in place, she felt herself picked up and dumped into the van, coming into contact with a body. Please, Lord, save me! Please! was her heart's cry as she felt the van pick up speed and disappear into the growing darkness.

Chapter 22

Caleb stood in the parking lot in front of Smitty's warehouse, Eddie on one side of him, Smitty on the other, watching as Frankie and a team of officers headed for the front door, Smitty's keys and the security password in hand, red and blue lights playing across their grim faces. Abe and his team stood nearby. Abe had been unable to raise either Micah or Joseph and he didn't like the feeling that he was getting.

Minutes later, Wilson came running back out and towards them. "We've found Micah. He's down and we can't get him roused. So far, no sign of Joseph or Leah." He turned to Abe. "Frankie wants Matt to come in and look at Micah."

Matt headed for the building, fear in his heart. How bad was Micah hurt and where was Joseph?

Wilson headed back with Matt, Eddie beside him.

"What do we know so far, Wilson?" Eddie's voice was hard.

"Not a lot. It looks as if Leah was closing up and something happened in the warehouse." They looked up as an officer approached.

"What did you find?" Eddie asked as he got near them.

"We've found a weapon but no one around it. I've posted someone there until we can get the crime scene team in. It looks like it fell or was kicked, from where it's lying."

"Show me." Eddie ordered as he followed the officer.

"Micah's this way, Matt. I've put in a call for the town paramedics, but we can't let them in yet, not until we've cleared the warehouse and that's going to take some time."

Matt nodded, eyes scanning the area as he walked towards the back of the warehouse. Where was Joseph and Leah? Had their fears be realized?

He dropped to his knees beside Micah. His hand shaking, he reached to check for a pulse. Breathing easier when he found it, he quickly checked him for injuries, stopping when he felt the lump on the back of the head.

He could see the dark of blood congealing on it. There didn't seem to be other injuries, but he would wait until he could move him safely with the help of the town paramedics.

Wilson approached, Dave Allison and his partner Tom, the paramedics, behind him.

"How is he, Matt?" Dave's question cut through the stillness in the building.

"He's alive. He's been knocked down, has a head injury. I don't see anything else."

Matt stood and stepped back as the two paramedics went to work, his eyes moving around the area. Abe stopped beside him, grim lines on his face, eyes on Micah.

"What's the word on him, Dave?"

"Like Matt said, a head injury. I don't see anything else. We're just getting ready to take him in. Who's riding with us?"

"Matt can. I want the others here for now. I'll catch up with you later. Matt, make sure you stay with him, no matter what they say. Use our government security contract if necessary. Don't let him out of your sight. If he saw anything, they may come after him again." Abe turned to leave, then stopped. "No sign of either Joseph or Leah that you've heard of?"

Matt shook his head. "I haven't heard anything, Abe, but I was concentrating on Micah."

Abe nodded, then headed for where he could see Eddie, Frankie and Caleb. He didn't like the grim looks on their faces.

Caleb turned as Abe came near. "We haven't found any sign of either Joseph or Leah." He handed Abe the evidence bag containing the weapon. "Do you know if this is Joseph?"

Abe studied it. "If I can take it out of the bag and check the serial number, I can tell you for sure." He took the latex gloves handed him and slipped them on, then pulled the weapon from the bag, and checked the serial number. His face tightened into sterner lines. "It's Joseph's. But where is he?"

"He's not in the building, Abe, nor is Leah." Caleb stared around, then turned to walk back through the warehouse. "The officers have searched just about everywhere they can."

Abe shook his head. "That's what I thought you would be saying. Matt's on his way in with Micah. I told him not to leave his side."

Caleb nodded. "I'll send in some officers as well. So far, he's the only one who knows what happened here."

Smitty watched, his heart dropping, as Caleb and Abe walked towards him. Rory stood beside his father, hand on his shoulder.

"Caleb?" Smitty's question hung in the air.

"She's not in there, Smitty. I'm sorry." Caleb stopped in front on him, eyes staring into the distance. "In my wildest dreams, I never thought this would happen. There was always the possibility of this, but I had prayed that with two of Abe's men with her, she would be safe."

Smitty nodded. "Now what?"

Caleb's eyes came back to Smitty. "We keep looking through the warehouse for signs of what happened. We pray Micah knows what happened. And we wait. That's what the tough part will be, the waiting."

Smitty nodded, then turned to walk away, his steps heavy, shoulders bowed. Rory kept his hand on his father's shoulder. "I now need to go talk to Emily. I don't know how to tell her."

"Smitty, wait. Take Ben and Marg with you." Abe spoke from behind him.

"That will help. Ben will be able to walk you through what we'll be doing now to find them."

Smitty's steps hesitated, then he nodded.

Abe shook his head, frustration and anger coursing through him. Why, Lord, he questioned, why did this have to happen? We had her safe and now this. Please, dear Lord, bring them both back to us.

"You're sticking around for a while, Abe?" Caleb quiet question cut through his thoughts.

"I am, Caleb. So are the fellows. If you need our help, just ask." Abe sighed. "I have to change our training schedule for next week, and that will take some work. Micah's not going to be up to training on the computer, and Joseph's missing. We'll pick up as best we can."

"If our people can help, let me know."

Abe nodded. "I'll pull in Gideon and Sidney to help. Ben will too." He stopped, his mouth drawing into a tight line. "How did they know it was just the three of them? Who told them?"

"That's what Eddie will be working on. There'll be a whole team on it now, not that

that's any consolation, Abe. We'll do our best to find them and get them home."

"The government's just going to love this. They wanted to stick her away in a safe house, and I wouldn't let them."

"She wouldn't have gone, Abe. She'd have run first." Caleb turned to watch the warehouse again. "She would have been gone before they even got to town to get her."

Abe drew a deep breath, then blew it out. "I know she would have. All my guys would have helped her to go and then kept quiet on where she was. Ian was ready to get the plane out yesterday and fly her somewhere, he had a feeling something was coming.

"I'm heading in to see how Micah is. Let me know where you are with the investigation and if I can do anything."

Micah's eyes opened slowly and then closed again the pain he felt. He couldn't remember what had happened and didn't know where he was. As he opened his eyes carefully again, he saw the sterile room he was in, the equipment around him, and then groaned. Movement to his right caught his attention, and he carefully turned his head. Matt stood there, concern etched on his face.

"Micah, how's the head?"

"Don't even ask. Where am I?"

"In the Emergency room. What do you remember?"

Micah's eyes slid shut. "I don't know."

Matt waited for Micah to speak again, then realized he had drifted off again. He turned as Abe entered the room.

"How is he?" was Abe's first question.

"He was just awake and is in a lot of pain. I asked if he could remember anything and he was out again before he could say."

Abe nodded. "I just spoke with the doctor. He's got a concussion for sure. They're going to keep him overnight to monitor him. I take it you're staying?"

Matt nodded. "I am. Who else will be?"

"Luke will be at the door. Nathaniel will be in the waiting room. We'll trade off part way through the night." Abe studied the still form of Micah. "I just wish it had been different, Matt. I just wish we could have gotten this guy before it got to this point."

"I know, Abe. Everyone involved was hoping the same thing. Murphy would tell you God's got it."

Abe gave a small smile and agreed, just as there was a commotion at the door. He strode to it and pulled it open, then sighed. Of course, the government guys would be here.

"Finlay, what's going on?" The senior official tried to force his way into the room, but Luke and Nathaniel moved in to block him. "Get them out of here. I want to talk to that guy in there."

Abe moved to the corridor, knowing that everyone around would hear. Good, he thought. Let them.

"You're not going anywhere near him. You have absolutely no authority to talk to him or even be near him. Leah was under our care, not yours. Her father no longer delivers for the government." Abe's voice held his barely controlled anger. "I have spoken with your supervisor, and I will again to let him know just what has gone down."

Spluttering in anger, the man backed away. "You'll not get another government contract, Finlay, when I get done with you."

"Try it. I think you'll find out differently, considering my security clearance and contacts go a whole lot higher than even your supervisor."

The man looked shocked, then turned and almost ran from the hallway. Abe watched him go, then turned to Luke and Nathaniel. "Why do they always think they know best?"

Luke shrugged. "Because they're the government. They forget who pays their wages, don't they? How's Micah?"

Abe shook his head. "Matt said he was awake for a minute but didn't remember anything. I want you at his door, Luke, until one of us comes to relieve you. Nathaniel, you'll be in the waiting room. Murphy and Ian will be in midway through the night to relieve you, if they wait that long. Matt's in the room with him. Caleb's sending some officers over as well."

"What's the word on the investigation at the warehouse?" Nathaniel's voice was quiet.

"I haven't heard anything more, other than what's we've already talked about. Somehow I don't think they'll find much there."

"Just a thought, Abe." Luke was still staring down the way the man had run. "How do we know it's not him or one of the government guys setting this up?"

Abe nodded. "I've thought of that. Gideon's working that angle for me."

Chapter 23

Leah felt herself pulled to her feet and dragged from the van. She stumbled, not being able to see where she was walking. She felt herself pulled up some stairs and then shoved into a room, hitting the wood floor hard. Stunned, she lay there, waiting for what, she wasn't sure. She heard movement and then the sound of a body hitting the floor near her. Who was it, she wondered? Joseph? Micah? Someone else?

Please, dear Lord, protect us from whoever these people are. Let no harm come to us. Keep up secure in Your hands. She listened for footsteps and heard none. As she reached for her blindfold, a hand came down on her arm and yanked her to her feet, shoving her into a chair. Head spinning, she slumped, not knowing what was going on. A flash of light came around her blindfold, then she heard heavy footsteps crossing the creaky floor and the sound of a door slamming shut and locking. What was that? she wondered.

Waiting for what she wasn't sure of, she prayed as she had never prayed before. *If this is to get my attention, Lord, You've got it. If this is to make my trust in You grow, that's working.*

She carefully raised her hands to her face and undid the gag and then the blindfold, blinking in the dim light coming through the dirt-encrusted windows. Wrists to her mouth, she bit at the knot in her bindings until she felt it give. Continuing to work at them, she finally had the hands frees. Rubbing her scraped and bleeding wrists, she looked around, trying to find a way out.

She gasped as her eyes lit on the figure on the floor and she flew from her chair to kneel beside it. Gently she rolled the figure to its back.

"Joseph! Oh, Joseph, what did they do to you?" Her eyes dimmed with tears as she studied the unconscious figure in front of her. Then, she felt for a pulse. Eyes sinking closed, she sat back. He was alive. Now she had to figure out how to get both of them out of there.

She drew back her fingers at the feel of wetness from the back of his head. *They hit him,* she thought. *They hit him and now he's bleeding. Dear Lord, let him be okay. I don't* think I could take it if he isn't. You alone know how much he has come to mean to me over the last few days and weeks. She sat as close to him as she could, hand resting on his chest, and looked around once again. There was only the one door in and out.

Eddie looked up from the paperwork he was reading as Caleb entered the conference room. Once again, it was a hive of activity as they desperately searched for Leah and Joseph. Without a lot to go on, it was almost fruitless.

Caleb sat beside Eddie, fatigue evident in his every movement. He didn't think he had slept much in the last thirty-six hours and he needed some to keep alert. He searched the room and nodded. Eddie had assembled the best of the team there. Frankie was working with the crime team tech. Abe sat on the other side of Eddie, watching as well.

"Where do we stand now, Eddie?"

Eddie shook his head. "About where we were the last time you asked. Without any new information, we just don't have enough to try and find them." He looked behind him, then back at Caleb. "Jace called a while ago. He's on his way over. He found something in that research he was doing on Smitty's employees."

"Let's pray that it leads to them." Caleb turned as the door behind him opened, and an officer ushered in Smitty. Caleb was on his feet and at Smitty's side, dismayed at the look on his face.

"Smitty?" Caleb's quiet question brought Smitty's head up.

"I got this, Caleb." Smitty's hand was shaking as he handed over his phone. "They want a trade, but I don't know what they want to trade her for."

Caleb's eyes searched Smitty as he took the proffered phone, Eddie beside Smitty directing him to a chair. Eddie's eyes met Caleb's and they both knew they were working with a time crunch now.

Caleb looked down at the picture in the text message. A bound and gagged Leah was there, along with the message that the kidnappers would be in touch in an hour with instructions. He forwarded the message to Frankie, who turned to stare at him after he read it, then turned back to the tech. They would track it down if at all possible.

"Smitty?" Caleb's voice brought his head up. "Have you any idea who?"

Smitty shook his head. "No, I don't. I wish I did. Find my little girl, Caleb. Find her and bring her back." His head dropped back down as his emotions overcame him.

Caleb looked around and seeing Wilson, beckoned him over. A few quiet words, and Wilson was leading Smitty from the room. He would stay with him until this was resolved, Caleb knew. Emily and Rory would also have protection.

Micah watched as Matt paced the hospital room, knowing they were all frustrated.

"I'm telling you, Matt. I didn't see a thing. Joseph went to investigate a noise we heard, I had Leah tucked away, and then nothing. There had to be someone in the warehouse. I found a door sensor that indicated the door wasn't closed, but it was. Leah had us check it."

Matt spun. "If someone was there, why didn't the security system alert you to that?"

"Whoever it was had to have had an employee badge. Leah said that's the only way the security system wouldn't alert to intruders. She hadn't had a chance to set it for the night when this went down." He laid his head back on the pillow, his headache building again. "I need out of here and to a computer. I need to search their system."

"That's not happening, Micah. The doctor won't let you near one."

Micah threw back the covers and sat up, the room spinning for a minute. "Grab me my clothes. I'm out of here."

Matt shook his head but handed Micah his clothes.

"Where are you wanting to head?"

"Where's Abe at?"

"At the police department. Is that where you want to go?"

Micah nodded. "I can access their security system from there. Joseph connected it to our system when this all started just in the event something like this happened. No word yet?"

Matt shook his head as his hand went out to steady his friend. "Not yet. But then I've been stuck here with you all night."

Abe turned as he heard his name called quietly, then stood and approached Micah.

"Sprung yourself out, did you? How's the head?"

Micah squinted through bleary eyes. "It's fine. Is there a computer I can use? Something's bugging me about last night. Leah hadn't set the security system for the night, but there was no warning someone was in the warehouse. She said the system alerts even in the daytime if someone is out there without an employee badge?"

Abe's eyes met Caleb's and then slid shut. "Someone who works for Smitty did this?"

Micah nodded, a grim look in his eyes. "That's what I'm afraid of. So, which can I use, Caleb?"

Caleb pointed to a free terminal and then watched as Micah slowly lowered himself to a chair. "He shouldn't be here, Abe."

"No, he shouldn't be. He should be on bed rest." Abe sighed. "But these guys are so close to one another, they'll do anything they can. You can bet that the others are out there searching right now."

Wilson came back in at that point, Jace from Tracker's beside him. "Caleb, Jace has some information I think you need to hear."

"Jace, what do you have?"

Jace looked around the busy room, then asked, "Is there somewhere we can talk in private? You and Abe and I?"

Caleb nodded, then led the way to his office, closing the door behind them. "What do you have?"

Jace handed over the papers he had been holding. "I can tell you without a shadow of a doubt it's not the government contract that brought this on."

Caleb's hand stilled as he took the papers. "It's not?" When Jace shook his head, he continued, "So what is is?"

"I tracked through all the employees. There are two who have been with Smitty for about six months. They have criminal backgrounds that were so well hidden it took time to trace them. It is a pure fluke that I came upon them."

"Not a fluke. God." Abe's comment stopped Jace, who then nodded.

"Absolutely. I also found out that these two men had dummy badges made up that match theirs. The owner of that business has to be involved."

Caleb nodded. "We'll bring him in. What else?"

"I have tracked through what I can of the companies Smitty deals with. I have narrowed it down to this one."

Caleb took the name, then shook his head. "It all fits, you know. We'll bring in the owner of that business as well." He looked up at Jace. "Once again, my thanks, Jace. You have gone above and beyond."

"No thanks are needed, Caleb. We just want to help get Joseph and Leah back home."

Abe watched as Jace left, then turned to Caleb. "Where now?"

"We bring in these two business owners and then track down those two employees. Just pray that we make it in time." Caleb stood to leave the office but stopped as his phone rang.

When he hung up, he turned to Abe. "Micah tracked down something he needs us to see. Your guy's good."

Abe smiled. "He's one of the best I know. All my guys are."

"They are. Now, you've got people coming in next week. Are you going to need any help in the training?"

Abe sighed. "That's a real possibility. Do you have someone you can send it to help? Micah's not up to training on computers at the beginning of the week and with Joseph missing, I'm short. I had planned on calling in Gideon and going to Ben too."

"Sounds like you have it covered." Caleb shoved open the door to the conference room and studied the white board, confident that progress had been made while they had been meeting with Jace.

"What do you have, Micah?" Abe dropped into the chair beside him. "Beside a blinding headache?"

Micah squinted at him. "I found out when they came in to the warehouse. It was through that door that we had the issue with. Four of them came in, all with badges."

Caleb nodded. "We just found out that two employees are involved and that they had two additional badges dummied up. We're working on that angle." He looked around. "Can you tell names from that or draw up pictures?"

"Check your printer over there. I just sent the information there." Micah sat back, eyes closed, pain evident on his face.

"Micah, come on. We need to get you out of here." Abe reached to draw him to his feet.

"I'm not leaving, Abe, not until I know that what I found brings them home."

Matt stood behind him. "Maybe we can find a place for you to stretch out here somewhere for a while."

Caleb sent them to his office, knowing that Micah would just sit in a chair somewhere until he knew that the information was profitable to the investigation.

Chapter 24

Joseph's senses picked up on a presence near him. His head wasn't clear enough to understand what had happened. He moved involuntarily and stopped at the pain from his head. A soft hand touched his face and he could hear a soft voice calling his name. He knew the voice, but the darkness closed in again before he could respond.

Leah watched as Joseph had roused then disappeared back into the darkness of unconsciousness. She sat, waiting for what she couldn't tell. She wasn't even sure how long it had been since they had been taken. Micah drifted into her thoughts, and she prayed that he was alive and okay. Why, Lord? she questioned once more before she drifted off to sleep, her head dropping.

The door opened, and the man stood staring at the two in the room. He walked over, footsteps heavy, and hauled Leah to her feet and shoved her once more into the chair. Her eyes blinded by the light he shone in them, she didn't see the paper he shoved into her hands. Disoriented, she blinked, trying to focus as once again a photo was taken of her and the man strode from the room, locking the door behind him.

She slumped to the floor again, crawling over to Joseph. She just didn't understand what was happening. She laid her hand on his shoulder, then laid down beside him. I am just so tired, she thought, I'll lay here for a minute.

Caleb turned as Wilson came towards him, phone in hand, his heart sinking at the sight. "Another message?"

Wilson nodded. "Smitty's had about as much as he can take. Another message and I don't how he'll take it."

Caleb reached for the phone. "We need to keep his phone. He doesn't need to see the pictures or hear the details of what the message is." Caleb stared down at the screen. "It's been what six hours since the last text? What happened to their hour?"

Wilson nodded. "That's my question, Caleb. Have they had any luck finding this guy?"

Frankie spoke from behind him. "Not yet. Whoever set this up knows what they're doing."

Caleb nodded. "Go to Tracker's if you have to. Jace said they're willing to do what they can. They have resources we don't. If Micah was up to it, I'd ask him."

Frankie nodded and headed off to find Jace. Caleb watched him go, then turned once again to Smitty's phone and read the note: "Two hours. We want that package from Wholesale Gems. Deliver it to us and your daughter lives."

"Not the kind of message any parent would want to receive." Caleb sent Wilson on his way and turned to find Eddie. "What do we know about Wholesale Gems?"

Eddie shot him a look, then looked back at the papers he had been reading. "I was just looking up that company. They have a long history of dealing with Smitty's but lately the company has been on shaky financial ground. The founder died, and the son took it over, pretty much running it into the ground. Rumour has it that they were expecting a shipment of a rare stone, but I can't confirm that." Eddie stopped, staring into the distance, then brought his eyes back to Caleb. "Is this what it's all about?"

"It's beginning to look that way." He turned as he heard Abe's voice raised a bit in anger. "Abe's letting the government know to back off?" Eddie nodded. "That's going to go over well, I suspect. Back to this. Do what you can to confirm this, then go talk to Smitty and find out if they really do have a parcel on site for them."

As he turned away, he had another thought. "Send someone to find the owner of that business and get them in here. Maybe that's how we can find those two."

Abe returned to the room, an angry look on his face. Caleb stared at him. They had been friends for years and he didn't think he had ever seen Abe with a look like that on his face. "I take it that conversation went about that well."

Abe gave a tight nod. "Where are we now, Caleb, and what can my guys do?"

"Smitty had another message, giving us two hours to come up with a shipment from his warehouse. I've sent officers to bring in the owner of a gem company." He looked around at the activity. "I wish Micah was up and on his feet. I could use his help."

"What do you need, Caleb?" Micah's voice behind him caused him to spin around. Micah looked steadier, although still pale.

"I need you to do some research we don't have the capability to do. Here's the name of the company and the owner. Jace is working on it as well.”

“Well, let’s see who finds it first.” Micah gave a quick grin and then sat at the computer, his fingers flying before he was even properly seated.

A few minutes later, he called Abe over, handing him a paper he had been taking notes on. Abe questioned him, then turned and left the room, Caleb’s eyes following him, then turning back to Micah.

Abe gathered up the five men he had around and leading the way, left the building. Eddie had followed and stood watching as they talked, then headed for their vehicles. He must have a lead that he’s not sure on, Eddie thought, and turned back to the conference room. Please, Lord, find them for us.

The activity in the room continued to increase as it approached the two-hour deadline. Caleb shot a glance at the clock, then walked over to Micah.

“What do you have, Micah?”

“A lot and Jace has confirmed it with me.” Micah pointed at the printer. “There’s your information: names, addresses, connections. It should be enough for search warrants, if not arrest warrants.”

"Are you serious? You've been able to find all that in that short of time?"

Micah nodded. "I'll keep working. Abe went to check out a lead I gave him a while ago. I haven't heard anything back from him, but I have done some more research. That building I think they're in is slated for demolition. I just pray it's not down already."

"What's the address?" Caleb reached for it and then sent a man on the run to the dispatch area to send officers there. "I pray we get there in time." He looked around for Frankie and Eddie and calling them, headed for the door. A quick word to Wilson kept Wilson with Smitty.

"Where are we heading, Caleb?" Frankie was puzzled, to say the least. They had less than thirty minutes left before the deadline and Caleb had pulled them out of the room.

"Micah came up with an address that fits. We're on our way there, I just hope in time. The building was to be torn down over the weekend."

Caleb didn't see the looks that passed between the men with him. Eddie's eyes closed in prayer. Not this close, Lord, please let them live.

Abe watched the building in front of him. It was derelict, almost falling down. A piece of heavy machinery sat in front of it, ready for its task on the morrow. Lord, if they're in there, we need to go in now. He turned as the five men with him approached, ready for work.

"Nathaniel, can you get up in the driver's seat there and watch?" Nathaniel nodded and headed for his spot. As the sniper on the team, he needed a good high place to perch. "Here's what we'll do. Luke, Murphy, head for the front door. Matt, stay near Nathaniel for now and be ready to come when I call. Ian, you're with me to the back. Before we go, let's pray."

Matt stood in the shadow of the machinery and watched, eyes alert. He knew the chance of the two being in there was slim but he prayed they were and that his team was in time.

Joseph rolled to his side once again, eyes fluttering and then staying open. He tried to focus, then closed his eyes once again. After a few minutes, they opened again, and this time stayed focused. Where was he, he wondered? He sat up, careful to keep his balance as the room spun. Then looking around, he assessed where he was.

His eyes lit on Leah lying there and he edged over and touched her.

Leah felt the touch and laid still, playing possum as her brother would say, until she realized she wasn't being hauled to her feet once again. She moved cautiously and turned, facing Joseph.

"Joseph! Are you okay?"

"I would nod, but I think my head would fall apart. Where are we?"

Leah shrugged. "I have no idea and I have no idea what day it is." She studied him, noting that he seemed to be okay. "What say we make a break for it?"

He looked at her, then around. "How? I would think the door is locked."

"It is but do you have a pocket knife?"

He nodded and reached for it. "They didn't take anything from us, other than our phones?"

"That would be the size of it." She took the knife and headed for the door, working on the hinge pins.

Joseph rose and in an unsteady manner, approached. "Ah! Now I see what you're after. Are they working loose at all?"

She nodded. "If you could lean on the door for me while I work on the top one."

Joseph held out his hand. "Let me. I'm taller and it will be easier."

Hinge pins out, Joseph worked to free the door, catching it before it fell on them. Setting it to the side, he peeked out the door.

"It sounds all quiet. Let's move. I want to be out of here before anyone comes back."

Moving quietly, they headed for the stairs, stepping around the debris lying on the floor and then on the stairs.

"Which door, Joseph?"

"The back, I think. They would expect us to try and leave through the front." He grabbed her hand and pulled her after him, hearing a soft noise at the front door. He hesitated for a minute, then continued.

Abe shoved himself up against the back wall of the house as he saw the door knob turning, weapon in hand, ready to act. Ian copied his stance on the other side of the door. As it opened, Abe reached for the arm of the man exiting, then stopped.

"Joseph!" His exclamation was quiet but joyful.

"Abe?" Joseph looked around. "Ian? What are you two doing here?"

"Looking for you two." Then speaking into his radio, he said, "Hey, guys, fade back to the van. We've got them." Leading the way, Abe hurried for the van they had left on another street. Ian was behind them, eyes watchful, concern on his face for Joseph and Leah.

Chapter 25

Caleb pulled his phone from his holster as he sped towards the house.

"Caleb, we have them!" Abe's voice rang over the airwaves. "We're heading back to your department."

Caleb slowed his vehicle and turned back towards the building. "I'll get the details when I get back. Dispatch, send cruisers to watch that building but I don't want any man or car visible. Got that?"

Confident that his orders would be carried out, Caleb led the way back into the building.

"Where's Abe?" he found Wilson still with Smitty.

Wilson shrugged. "I saw him come in but I'm not sure where he got to."

"Find him and bring his team to the smaller conference room, if they're not there already." He watched as Wilson left, then sent Eddie and Frankie back to the larger room. "You know what we need now. Find the information and get us the warrants we need."

He then turned to Smitty. Smitty slumped in his chair, eyes closed, devastation in his very demeanour.

"Smitty." Caleb touched his shoulder, causing him to jump. "Smitty, come. Up with you and come with me."

Smitty looked up through blurring eyes. "You have news?"

Caleb nodded. "Come with me." He led him to the room, opening the door.

Abe's men turned as Smitty entered, then parted as he walked forward. Seeing Leah, he was across the room and had his daughter in his arms before anyone could say anything. Leah clung to her father as sobs wracked her body. More than one of the men had tears in their eyes as they looked away. Caleb motioned for Abe and the two left the room.

"Talk to me, Abe. Tell me what happened."

"Micah came up with that address but wasn't sure if it was even valid given it was a derelict building. Rather than pull your men in on a wild goose chase, I took mine. We met them coming out of the building as we were ready to go in. I haven't asked them what happened. That's up to you."

Caleb nodded, then looked past Abe and grimaced. "I thought you made it clear to the government that it wasn't their delivery."

"I did." Abe spun, then turned around again. "Get us out of here before he sees us, Caleb. I'm in no mood to go over and over what he wants."

"Not a problem. I'll head him off, you disappear out the back door. Just be careful. They're likely watching the road to your place."

Abe nodded. "I suspect they are. They're refusing to believe it's something other than that contract. Catch up with us tonight, and I'll have those two ready to give statements. Which of your men do you want to come with us?"

"Eddie, I think. I can pull him from the investigation. He can get their statements too. It won't look odd if he's at your place, given you're related."

"That's true." Abe disappeared through the door as Caleb walked towards the front of the building, mind racing as to how to duck the questions he knew were coming.

Leah sat back in the van, her father beside her and Joseph on her other side, grasping the hands of each man. She still couldn't believe that they had just been able to walk right out of that building and into Abe's care. *Thank you, Lord. You kept us safe and secure once again and brought us to safety.*

Abe knew that no one could see into the back of the van and that it was now dark. He worried though about how to get them into the house as the motion sensor lights would trigger.

"Take them in through the tunnel, Abe." Micah's voice was quiet from beside him.

Abe turned, thoughtfully regarding him. "I think you're right. We can park in such a way that no one would see where they were going. If you all scatter to your homes and then regroup at mine, it won't look odd. Did you get that, Ian?"

Ian, the driver, nodded. "I did. I think it will work. Their adventure is far from over though, not until we get these guys."

Abe nodded as he looked behind him. The second van followed and then parked in a way to block sight from the road to the first van. Smitty, Leah and Joseph were hustled from the van, Joseph leading the way to the entrance to the tunnel.

"This is interesting," Smitty commented.

"It is." Joseph grabbed a flashlight from a shelf and clicking it on, led the way. "It's part of our safe room/escape route from Abe's house. We had to use it with Adriel not long ago, only we went out instead of in. No one knows it's here."

By the time they reached the basement of the house and Joseph led them up the stairs, Abe had closed up the house with only minimal lights on. He pointed quietly to the kitchen and Joseph headed that way, grateful to be sitting down again. Matt followed, setting his kit on the table, and reaching to assess Joseph's head.

"How's the headache?"

"Not bad, all things considered. The lump doesn't even really hurt either."

"It will tonight when you're trying to sleep." Matt turned to Leah. "Are you okay? Did they hurt you in anyway?"

She held up her arms. "Other than the abrasions from the rope, I'm fine. Just really tired and thirsty."

Matt took a look at her wrists, applying a soothing cream and then wrapping them. "They're okay but I'll look at them in the morning. No other injuries that need medical attention, you two?"

Joseph and Leah stared at each other, then at Matt. "No." Joseph was puzzled. "Just what you've seen. Micah seems to have gotten the worst of it."

"I think he did. It was the angle they caught him at that did that."

Smitty sat beside his daughter, fatigue weighing him. "I need to let Emily and Rory know that Leah's safe."

Abe turned. "That's a problem, Smitty. We're trying to keep it quiet until we have the men in custody." He thought about it. "Tell you what. Have Emily and Rory go to Ben and Marg. I'll talk to Ben and he can let them know."

Smitty nodded. "That would work. Thanks, Abe." He went to pull out his phone. "I guess Caleb still has my phone, doesn't he?"

Abe turned back to Smitty, a strange look on his face. "That he does. Tell me, Smitty. Did you ever leave your phone anywhere in the warehouse where someone had access to it?"

Smitty shrugged. "It's always a possibility. I do have a habit of leaving it in any one of the offices and then have to track it down." His voice died away, and he stared back at Abe, his face starting to pale. "Are you saying they're using my phone in some way?"

"It's possible. Micah checked. The number you were getting the messages on wasn't your work phone. It was your personal phone. Your staff could very well have that." Abe watched as dawning comprehension spread across Smitty's face.

"You're telling me it's an employee who did this?"

Abe nodded. "Caleb's men together with Jace from Tracker's have tracked down two fairly recent employees. I hate to tell you this too, but they had dummy employee badges made up as well, all in preparation for this. There's been a lot of planning involved."

Smitty's eyes closed. As Leah laid her hand on her father's arm, his eyes opened.

"I'm sorry, Leah and Joseph. If only I had known."

"No one knew, Dad, no one at all. They covered it so well we never knew we couldn't trust any one of our staff."

Abe handed Smitty his phone, then turned as Ian set food on the table. "We need to eat, then Eddie will need to get your statements you two. For tonight, everyone's in the house. Gideon and Rebecca are away until Monday."

"Has the government given up, Abe?" Joseph's question stopped everyone's movement and they all looked at Abe.

"No, unfortunately they haven't. Caleb was heading them off as we went out the back door." Abe looked around at them all. "I don't think it will stop until we bring in the ones truly responsible and that's going to take a few days. Eddie, was Caleb working on your warrants?"

Eddie nodded. "He was. With the information from Jace and Micah, we should have enough. It's a matter of getting a judge to sign off on the warrants and then serving them."

Leah's head was nodding and she laid it against Joseph's shoulder, barely able to keep her eyes open. Smitty looked at her, then moved his chair back. Joseph was ahead of him, scooping her into his arms and heading down the hall to her bedroom, Smitty on his heels. A quiet word and Smitty pulled the blankets back, pulling them back up over his daughter and tucking her in. He stood and watched her sleep, sorrow in his heart at what she had faced. He dropped a quick kiss on her head and then sought the arm chair near the bed, settling down for the night. He was not letting her out of his sight.

Joseph pulled the door partway closed, then headed back to the kitchen. He could feel the anger building in him, even though he knew it was a useless emotion.

"Now what, Abe? Where do we go?" Joseph sat, eyes on his team leader.

"We leave it now for Caleb to work through. If they need our help, we'll give it. Eddie here wants to get your statement. He'll get Leah's later." Abe sat, a cup of coffee in his hands that he was twisting as he thought. "Walk us through what happened, what you can remember."

Joseph shrugged. "I don't remember much. I can remember Leah locking the cash away in the safe, then heading back to the warehouse. Next thing, I remember is waking up in that building, then Leah asking me for a knife."

"A knife?" Eddie's question was what they were all thinking.

Joseph nodded. "A knife. We used it on the hinge pins to get the door off." He shook his head. "They took our phones but didn't search any further. Who does that?"

"Someone who isn't a criminal obviously." Eddie reached for his phone, then excused himself.

Abe watched as Joseph leaned his head onto his hand. This wasn't him. He finally reached over and shook his shoulder. "Joseph, go on. Lay down in the living room. Eddie can get your statement in the morning. You've given us the basics, so we're good."

Joseph nodded as he stumbled to his feet and headed for the other room, not seeing Matt on his heels, watchful for any signs of distress.

It will be a long night, Lord, Abe thought. *Bring healing and wisdom to us.*

Chapter 26

Leah stirred early the next morning, her eyes opening to see her father slumped in the chair near her bed, sound asleep. She smiled. Of course, he would be there. She rose, moving quietly, and headed for the kitchen. She needed her coffee and she hoped some would be ready. Her bare feet didn't make a sound as she entered the kitchen. It was empty, but the coffee was ready. Thank you whoever made it, she thought. A noise behind her had her spinning around, fear coursing through her, then relief as she saw it was Micah.

"Micah! How's your head?" Her voice was low.

"It's been better, but I'm glad to see you're up and about." He drew out a chair for her, then reached for a mug to pour his own coffee before sitting across from her.

"What happened, Micah?" She studied him as he took a sip of his coffee, grimacing at how hot it was.

"Abe can fill you in better than I can. I don't remember much past sticking you in the alcove, then waiting for Joseph to come back."

"He never come back, did he?" She stared across the room, lost in thought. "It had to be employees, Micah. That's the only way the alarm didn't go off."

"That's what we've figured out. Do you have any suspicions at all?" His eyes tracked behind her, watching Abe standing there, then came back to her face.

She nodded. "Two that are recent hires. I never liked them but couldn't put a finger on why I didn't. They always seemed to be too curious, too much in places they shouldn't be."

"Names, Leah?"

Abe nodded as he heard them. "Those are the names Caleb has, Leah. Do you know of any friends of theirs?"

She nodded and reached for a piece of paper. "Give Caleb these two," she commented as she wrote them out. "They've been hanging around and Dad has had to tell them to leave."

"Would your Dad remember them?"

She shrugged. "He might, but then he's always chasing people away." She thought a moment. "They were around on Tuesday. Ask Dad about the surveillance tapes. They would show up on the ones from the front of the warehouse." She turned to look at Abe. "What happens now, Abe?"

"For now, we keep it quiet that you're here. It will be a challenge as there's a new team coming in to train on Monday for four days." Abe walked away, lost in thought. Where could he stash those two? He turned to go back and find Ian. Maybe he would have an idea where he could fly them to.

Caleb looked back from the whiteboard in the conference room. Names had been added and erased from it as warrants were issued and served. The case was moving ahead, but he sensed there was still something else missing. Abe stood at the door, beckoning him.

"Abe, what brings you here?" Caleb pointed towards the front door.

"Thanks, Caleb. We need to talk in private and there's too much activity going on. How about a coffee at Mac's?"

Once settled into a booth at Mac's, Caleb watched his friend. Something was up and Abe wasn't quite sure how to express himself.

"Talk to me, Abe. What have you gone and done now?"

Abe sighed, his eyes drifting past Caleb to study the pictures on the wall at the back. He really wasn't interested in the scenes from the past winter and spring, but he was trying to gather his thoughts.

"Ian and I have come up with a plan we hope works. We need to get Joseph and Leah out of here for a week or two until you are at the point you really need them. I can manage without Joseph training next week." Abe quickly outlined his plan, Caleb asking questions and helping to refine it.

Finally, Caleb sat back. "It might work. Have you talked to Joseph and Leah?"

Abe shook his head. "I wanted to work it out with you seeing they're your witnesses."

Caleb nodded. "Who gets to break it to them?"

"I guess I do." Abe sat back as well, his eyes thoughtful. "I'm at a loss as to what to do with them otherwise, Caleb. If we keep them around here, they're in too much danger."

Caleb nodded. "So who's your other pilot?"

Abe shook his head. "I'd rather not say at the present. It's not someone you know."

Caleb slid from his seat and stood, stretching to work out some of the kinks he was developing from the stress. "Just keep me in the loop. Let me know if I can do anything. Tell Leah thanks for those other names."

Abe nodded, then scrubbed his face with his hands. This would be the hard part, convincing those two they needed to flee from town. He looked up as Mac slid into the seat across from him.

"Abe, you're puzzled and stressed. What can I do to help?" Mac watched as Abe shook his head and focused on him.

"I'm just trying to keep some people safe, and I'm not really sure that the plan I've come up with will work."

Mac looked at him. "Have you prayed about it and listened to what God has said?"

Abe nodded. "I have, and I know I need to follow what He's saying, but I'm still concerned."

Mac looked away for a minute, then looked back. He reached into his shirt pocket and pulled out a key, passing it across to Abe. "I have a cabin in the mountains that only Sue and I know about. None of the family have ever heard us talk about it. You can only get to it by air. Have Ian fly them in, if he can handle a float plane. There's no other way in by foot or vehicle."

Abe looked down at the key, then up at Mac, relief coursing through him. He knew Ian could handle the float plane, it was just a matter of getting him to one. "Mac, how do you do this? How do you know when we need something? You're always there."

Mac shrugged. "That is how God works through me, Abe. I ask for guidance, ask how I can help my friends, and He tells me." He pointed at the key. "This is one of those times. The only thing I ask is that you tell no one else where Ian's going. Send him in to see me and I'll give him a map. That map will need to be destroyed. This is a little area that Sue and I escape to every six months or so."

Abe watched as Mac stood and made his way back to the kitchen. Lord, I still don't understand how he knows. Thank you. He stood to leave, his eyes searching the cafe for someone who shouldn't be there. It was almost empty, just a few of the locals hanging around with their coffees. He could feel someone watching him but couldn't see anyone.

Ian stared at Abe as Abe handed him the key and Mac's message. "Are you serious? Mac mysteriously has this cabin we can go to for a week or so?"

Abe nodded. "He came to me just out of the blue and handed me that key. It sounds safe enough but go talk to him. He wants to give you a map of where it is." He looked around. "Where are Leah and Joseph?"

"In the back yard, I think. Leah was starting to get claustrophobic being inside all the time." Ian paused, deep in thought. "If I take them in, Abe, that leaves you short next week for training."

Abe shook his head. "Don't worry about it. We'll manage. Ben and Gideon are stepping in and Sidney has agreed to help. If anything, Caleb's willing to send in some people. If you're with those two, I think that should be enough. We just have to plan right in how to get you to where you need to be."

Leah and Joseph wandered the back yard, like others before them. Leah stared at the sky, the stars just beginning to peep out from the blackness. "When will it be over, Joseph? I'm tired of living like this."

Joseph watched what he could of her face. "Soon, I pray, Leah. Abe said Caleb's just about ready to wrap it all up." He stopped her forward movement with a hand to her arm. "How do you really feel about leaving for a bit?"

She shook her head. "I don't like it, Joseph. I feel like I'm running away and leaving everything to someone else to fix. That's not me. I need to be in control of my own life, and I'm not."

"None of us are right at the moment, Leah. I don't like this any more than you do. I lose out on training time next week, because of this. I can't court you like I want to, because of this. You can't spend time with your family, because of this. I can't go see my folks, because of this."

Leah looked at him, then began laughing. He stared at her in shock. "You sound like a broken record, Joseph, with your "because of this". Can you come up with another phrase, by chance?"

He started laughing as well, then turned as he heard footsteps approaching. "Abe, we were just talking about you. Where are we heading?"

Abe shrugged. "I have no idea. Mac has a cabin that he's willing to tuck you three away in for the week. Only Ian will know where it is." He looked between the two of them. "Are you two really okay to do this? If not, then we'll have to come up with something else."

"We're fine with it, Abe. Just so long as it's only for the week. Once the week is up, Ian needs to bring us back, regardless of whether Caleb is ready or not. I'll grant him one week." Leah stared back at Abe and he could see the peace she had reached in her heart about this.

He nodded. "All right, then. If things are ready from Ian's point of view, you'll leave tomorrow morning and be back one week from today. Ian will be staying with you. I wish I could send someone else, too."

"You can't really afford to lose even Ian, Abe, so don't worry about it. Just keep us in your prayers." Joseph watched as Abe went to speak, then turned and walked away. He felt Leah's arm slip through his and he reached for her hand.

"He's hurting, Joseph, and not just from what your team has been through. There's something else going on."

"I know there is, but he's kept everything so private, we don't know what it is."

Chapter 27

Three weeks later, Leah stood in the hallway aside the court room, surrounded by Matt, Ian, and Nathaniel, Abe standing a few feet away. She knew that Joseph had Luke, Micah and Murphy with him and that they had just left the building for their van. They had been called to give their testimony and were now heading out to Rebel's. She was worried. She could tell the men were uncomfortable and wanted to get her out of there.

Caleb's men had done their work and the arrests and investigations had brought the culprits to justice. What no one had counted on was that the mayor's wife would be involved. The evidence gathered was overwhelming against all of them. Caleb had indicated that they were likely facing long prison sentences.

Leah knew now that Davies' attack on her that day had been his own plan and that he had paid the ultimate price with his own death. His friends couldn't or wouldn't shed any more light on it. Leah figured they had been either too drunk or too high to know what he had planned. The government officials had finally realized that it wasn't their plans and armaments that the thieves were after and had disappeared now that the armaments had been assembled and shipped from town. The only thing they didn't know was who the man really was that had been in the hills or who had set the bomb in Davies' car.

Abe nodded at Ian, who touched Leah's arm. "We're ready to leave, Leah."

"Is this really necessary, Ian? Do I have to have you so tight around me?" Leah was starting to get angry that she had no freedom. She wanted to be free of all restraints and thought she would be now that the arrests had been made and the case was before the courts.

"Just for a day or two more, Leah. We just need to get you through to the end of the trials, and that will be by the end of the week." Ian's voice held a touch of sympathy, and she frowned at him.

Suddenly, Ian felt a hard shove from behind and he was falling forward, unable to catch himself or stop himself from taking

Leah with him. He wrapped his arms around her as best he could as they both tumbled down the few steps they had left to descend. He could faintly hear the yells and shouts around him. Then, his head thudded onto the cement sidewalk and he went limp, darkness descending in a swift curtain.

Leah lay still, Ian's arm still around her in protection. Matt was at their sides in an instant and he could hear the cries for the EMS to be called. Abe yanked the woman he had tackled to her feet and to the top of the stairs. Eddie stood there, shock in his face, then he was reaching for her.

"The mayor's daughter, is it?" Eddie was angry. Who knew how badly she had hurt the two. "I guess you'll be joining your mother in jail." He shoved her at an officer. "Book her for two counts of assault for now. We'll re-address the charges once we have Ian and Leah assessed by the physicians."

Abe turned and headed back down the stairs, eyes alert around him as he moved. His men were there, Joseph included, standing guard over their friends. Abe watched as the paramedics assessed, then headed the few short blocks to the hospital with Ian and Leah.

Joseph spun to confront him. Abe held up a hand to stop his words.

"We need to get you out of here, Joseph. We'll head for the hospital and talk there."

Joseph glared at him, then headed back for the van he had been in. Nathaniel watched, then turned to Abe.

"What happened? I didn't see anyone that looked suspicious."

"None of us did, Nathaniel. She just came out of the blue. It was the mayor's daughter." Abe looked around once again, still uncomfortable. "Let's get out of here. I don't like the feeling I have."

Smitty paced the waiting room, anxious for word on his daughter. Emily sat in one of the chairs, shredding the tissue she held in her hands, Rory beside her with his arm around her shoulders. Abe's men paced as well, moving in and out of the room, senses alert. They were angry, and Abe knew that, but also knew they were spending time in prayer for their friends. He turned to watch Joseph, slumped in a chair near Emily, head back against the wall. How close were he and Leah, he wondered? Something had changed between them when they had returned. When he questioned Ian, Ian just smiled and said to ask them. Abe figured another engagement was coming, but he wasn't sure of even that anymore.

Caleb stood at the entrance of the room and assessed what was going on. Then he crossed to Abe. "Got a minute, Abe? I need to talk with you?"

"Sure, as long as we don't leave here."

Caleb looked around, then pointed at a clear spot in the room. "Over there."

Once they were seated, Abe studied his friends' face. He didn't like what he saw. "Talk to me, Caleb. What's up?"

Caleb shook his head. "I just had to arrest the mayor for attempted murder of his son. When we went to talk to him about his daughter, he became enraged. He was involved in the scheme as well, from what the son had told us on the way into the house. The son knew absolutely nothing about it. He works away from here and doesn't have a lot of contact with his parents any more. When the mayor saw the son behind us, he tried to shoot him." Caleb stopped, pondering what had happened. "It's a shame, you know. They were well liked and did a lot for our town. But they were in financial difficulties. The wife had a gambling problem and they were trying to pay off the debt.

"We've no word on who set the bomb in the car, though. No one claims that responsibility. And your friend from the hill, we had to release him. He finally confirmed a name, but we can't track him to anyone involved in this."

Abe shook his head. "All this because of money. We have two friends hurt, lives have been upturned and destroyed, and for what? I will never understand this."

Caleb shook his head and then stood. "Come see me next week, Abe. We have some final paperwork to go over with you and Joseph and Leah when she's able. Any word yet?"

"Not yet. It feels like we've been here forever, but it's only been a couple of hours." He turned to Caleb. "Are they safe now, Caleb? Can I pull off the security from them?"

Caleb searched the room, his eyes stopping on each person in there. The Emergency Room was a busy place that day, but he knew just about everyone who was waiting. "I think you finally can, Abe. We have the ones involved, including the two employees and their friends. They turned quickly to give evidence against the mayor's wife." He walked away, burdens evident in his walk, but his back was straight as he knew where his strength came from.

Abe turned to find Joseph standing beside him. "Is it over, Abe?"

Abe nodded. "It is, Joseph. Caleb just wanted to let us know that they had to arrest the mayor as well."

"The mayor as well as his wife and daughter?" The shock Joseph felt played on his face. The rest of the team stood behind him and exchanged glances. "Did he say why?"

"He tried to shoot his own son." Abe looked around at his team, missing Ian standing there. "All this over a gambling debt, guys." He turned as he heard his name called and headed towards the nurse standing hear the reception desk.

"I'll take you back to Ian, Mr. Finlay. The doctor will be back with him soon and wants to talk to you." She looked past him at the six men standing right behind Abe and smiled. "I take it these fellows want to tag along?"

"If we can, Ma'am." Murphy spoke for the group.

"It's okay. The doctor said that you'd all want to come. Right there in Room 4."

Abe approached the bed where Ian lay, eyes closed, his face and arms scraped from the rough concrete. They all turned as the door open, and John Thompson, physician and friend, entered.

"How is he, John?" Abe asked once John had finished his assessment.

"No concussion, thankfully. Just a really bad headache. He's been awake on and off. We're keeping him in overnight." He looked around the room. "I understand his fiancée is on her way in?"

Abe nodded. "Lydia should be here soon, if not already." He looked at the men standing there. "Why don't you all take off? I'll let you know later how he is."

They nodded and with a last glance towards their friend, filed out. Murphy stopped as he saw Ian's fiancée, Lydia, hesitating at the entrance to the waiting room, fear on her face, and beckoned her to him.

"In here, Lydia. Abe's in with him." Murphy pushed the door to the room open, and watched as Lydia approached Ian, her hands going out to grasp his, Abe pulling a chair up for her to sit in.

Joseph slumped back into a chair, his mind racing. How was Leah? He didn't think there had been any word yet. He could still see her lying there, Ian's arm around her in protection, not moving. He looked up as he felt a hand on his shoulder. Smitty stood there, watching, then sat beside him.

"The doctor was out when you were in with Ian. They're moving her up to a room, Joseph. She'll be all right." Smitty leaned back. "Rory and Emily are heading up there now. I wanted to wait for you."

"For me?" Joseph turned to look at him.

Smitty smiled. "For you. I think you and Leah came to an agreement when you were away. Ian just smiles when we ask him. Leah walks away. You." Smitty shook his finger at Joseph. "Now, you, I haven't been able to corner to ask."

Joseph nodded. "First, her injuries?"

"Bruises, cuts, scrapes, a headache. Nothing serious, praise God, and thanks to Ian for his quick reflexes. Speaking of Ian, is he okay?"

Joseph nodded. "About the same as Leah. No concussion, which is a good thing." He studied his hands, not sure how to proceed with what he wanted to say.

"Spit it out, Joseph. That's usually the best way." Smitty had a twinkle in his eye. "Now, what is it?"

Joseph smiled at him. "You're right. We did come to an understanding. We haven't known each other all that long, but circumstances forced us to get to know one another quickly and, in a way, most dating couples never do. She agreed to be my bride, as long as you agreed to share her with me. She will not give up her family, she tells me."

Smitty smiled through tears. "We'll share, Joseph." He reached to shake Joseph's hand. "Welcome to the family, Joseph. Now, how be we go find your lady?" He stopped for a minute, then spoke again. "God protected you two over the last few weeks. We are blessed to have you with us, Joseph."

Three months later, Leah was on a search. Abe had told her that Joseph was up in the hills behind the compound but wouldn't tell her exactly where, just laughing when she pleaded with him to tell her.

Hearing a noise, she turned. Joseph stood, silent, just watching her and the sun reflecting off the face he loved. He held out his hand to her and pulled her with him to where he had been working.

Leah stopped, staring at the picnic dinner Joseph had prepared and spread out for them. She looked around at the view. The lake they loved was in front of them, the forest behind. Sitting down beside Joseph, their conversation was quiet as they ate.

"Any regrets, Leah?" Joseph didn't look at her as he asked.

She turned her head to watch his face. "Maybe some, Joseph, but they're mainly for lost opportunities and chances when I should have spoken up to witness for God during this and didn't. How about you?"

"The same, I guess I would have to say. When we were going through this, I never doubted for a minute that God would keep us secure in Him. No matter how it turned out."

Leah nodded. "I have to agree, Joseph. We take that security of His love and protection for granted. Even when the time comes to graduate to heaven, we know we have that in Him." She turned to look across at the lake, then back at him, to find him watching her.

"Leah, when you were in the hospital, your Dad spoke with me. Somehow, he knew we had reached an understanding. He's agreed to share you with me."

"Share me, huh?" She leaned against his arm. "I guess we could do that. I'm glad you who you are, Joseph, for your strong walk with God, your strength, your compassion. You're exactly who I need."

"And you are who I need, Leah. I can't begin to tell you how you compliment me and bring out the best. I strive every day, with God's help, to live up to the expectations you have for me and for us as a couple." He reached for her hand. "There is only one thing lacking, sweetheart." He reached into his shirt pocket and pulled out a ring. Leah focused on it. "This ring was my Mother's and was put aside by our parents for Ella when she graduated from college. She never got to that. They gave it to me, asking me to give it to you. It's your choice, sweetheart. If you want another, we can do that."

Leah looked down at the plain gold band with the simple rose sapphire entwined with white gold. She shook her head, and Joseph's hand moved backward until she stopped it with her hand on his. "No, Joseph. No other one. I would be honoured to wear the stone that would have been Ella's. I would like to have known the twin of the man I love."

Sealing their love with a kiss, they turned to watch the sun setting, knowing that God had led them to that point and that He would be the centre always of their home. They had been through an adventure they both prayed any children they had never had to go through, but God had been faithful through it all.

Dear Readers:

Thank you for picking up the story of Joseph and his lady, Leah. Like Leah, we have stresses and fears in our lives. We can either let them rule or we can let God have them. His desire is to keep us safe and secure in Him. When we turn these fears and stresses over to God, it doesn't mean we're done with them. It means that He will give us the peace we need to deal with them.

David, a man after God's own heart, must have felt the lack of security in his life so deeply, but he never once doubted Who God is or what He can do. That's what my aim was with this story - to draw the reader into a closer walk with God and to feel the security He provides us spiritually. He has set a road before us that we walk and only He know what lies ahead. That is where trust comes in.

As a child, I always felt safe and secure when Dad was home. Back in the 1960s, he would have to be away from home working from Monday to Saturday afternoon, leaving Mom, my sister and I home in the country. There was always a little bit of fear there, I must say, when Dad was away. When he was there, the safety and security surrounded us. I miss his wisdom and words so very much. And with my Dad being a carpenter, I saw him take out hinge pins all the time, so it's not a stretch for Leah to have come up with that.

May God lead and guide you and bless you richly as you put your hand into His and let Him lead.

Ronna